How To Fly
with Rocks in Your Pocket

Anna Beach

How To Fly
with Rocks in Your Pocket

Anna Beach

Cover Design by Gabby Edlin

Interior Graphic Design by Leandro Adad Jammal

First Printing: 2014

ISBN 978-0-9862133-0-4

http://www.annabeachwrites.com

This book is dedicated to my Kickstarter funders, without whom publication would not have been possible. These include, but are not limited to: the following:

Adie

Aimee Chapman

Amanda and Chris Beach, Family

Amanda Maria Edmonds

Amanda Voss, The Googler

Amelia Stefanac

Andrea and Tom Easley

Angela Schreiber

Becky and Mark Liefeld

Becky Crabtree

Betsy, Stephanie, and Roger

Betty Cheney, Pen Pal Extraordinaire

Bev Finley, Anna's Third Grade Teacher

Brianna

Brittany Cooperrider

Carolyn and Ed Beach

Christa, ADPi

Christen Kirk

Christi Wilkins, BFFL of the Author

Cousin Claire

Cousin Jennifer

Cynthia, Justin Timberlake's Biggest Fan

Danielle Gartner

Demaris LeBlanc

Dr. T

el Danielito

Elizabeth Roby

Ella Quiogue, The Most Awesome Filipino I Have Ever Met

Emily Beach

Eric and Frances Katz, The Cool Parents

Errol Weiss Schlabach, Musician and Composer

Georgia

Hilary Strimple

Hunter E Young

I-Win Rattanapian

Jane Wearstler

Janie Elizabeth Neyer, Tower 10 Floormate

Jeannette Maass

Jen

Jenn Cahill

Jessica Marcrum

John Garrity

Judy

Julia Smith

Julie Horger

Kate Anzinger, Cousin

Katie Anderson

Kay McCollough

Kristen Stevens

Lacey J. Davidson

Laura Green Gillis

Leandro Adad Jammal

Liana Began

Lindsay Hirschfeld Guzowski

Liz D

Lucy Wills

Meghan McLaughlin

Michael Dion

Michael Maslowski

Michelle

Miss Belinda

Molly Hoey

Mr. Hiroyuki Takeuchi

Ms. Elle Anzinger

Muiyuong Gamonpat Sanganunt

Nicole Rose

Patricia A. Davidson, My Godmother "Aunt Patty"

Rachel Cinlemis, Badass

Rachel Lee

Ramon Colon

Rev. Becky Piatt

RJ White

Ryan

Sally Alexander, Wittenberg ADPi

Samantha Grasso

Sandi and Scott Hoover

Sandra Ehirim

Sharel

Sir Rolando

Stephanie Brandstetter

Suzanne Klingelhoefer

The Brashear Family, Best Next Door Neighbors. Ever.

The Bredemeiers

Thorne N. Melcher, Goddess of Code

Tori Amicon, The Realest Person You Will Ever Meet

Walter Perfeito.

MAY

Lennie is a liar. Lennie was my best friend. When I knew her, she began each night with gin. She finished most evenings throwing up dinner in the bar washroom. She's pretty. She fucked boys who wouldn't call her pretty. She pretended that solo cups were Waterford crystal. She liked to pretend the wood laminate in our apartment was fine teak. She measured shots. She would blather on about how we were going to be friends forever. She never admitted regret. She never admitted defeat. She loved gin.

I think people who say they like the taste of gin are liars. That May, the last one when Lennie's presence in my life was constant, all I wanted was to forget the black. I wanted to forget the sad songs. I wanted to forget the speeches. I drank everything, gin included. I danced too close with strangers. I fell asleep on mismatched couch cushions. I forgot to remember. I remembered to forget. Change was ripe in the air. In time, Lennie—my fondness for her, her "love" of gin—would cease to have much bearing on my life. I didn't know that then, so I reacted as I always had. I never embraced feeling. I eschewed euphemism. I hated gin.

I've always felt as though I have been improperly expelled from some Victorian drama. Everything about my life that is asymmetric and modern would sound so much more beautiful if recounted in pleasant and flowery prose. Unfortunately, in the twenty-two years of life under my belt at the time, I'd never had the presence of mind to make statements like:

No! You, sir, are a scoundrel lower than a dog, or

My heart was an old piece of fruit forgotten in a drawer, shriveled, sad, malodorous, but never completely gone.

No. I was much more likely to say,

Fuck you, or,

I'm fine. I don't want to talk about it.

In playing back a small portion of my story, I may occasion-ally veer toward imagery or symbols in a misguided attempt to animate the mundane. I may become overzealous in my childish affection for dramatic prose spangled with cherry blossoms and moonbeams. I will certainly use language unsuitable for children. I may bring up memories that seem not to matter, people that seem not to matter. People like Lennie. Weaving together these odd fragments is the only way I know to be authentic, to tell how it was. Above all I want to tell how it was, because morning-afters don't happen in orchards on horseback. They happen, as they did that year, under fluorescent lighting, still holding a half-eaten tupperware container of mediocre pasta in hand, phone tucked into bra for easy access. This is America. Shoot someone if you don't like it.

I remember my alarm buzzing loudly that morning, waking up alone, brushing my teeth, taking my Prozac. I looked in the mirror at my plump, doughy, white face. Dry spittle had leaked from my mouth while I was sleeping. My bright blue eyes were lost in circles of smeared eyeliner and mascara; my greasy and disheveled blond hair was piled haphazardly on top of my head. I had managed to change into pajamas the night before in a drunken stupor: a tank top and leggings that hugged every expression of extra fat enfolded around the shape I would otherwise have been. That day was the last time I would examine myself in the peeling, dirty bathroom mirror, pulling and pinching at lumpy deposits I wanted to disappear. My eyes followed my reflection from my navel to my face, unimpressed. I wiped away wayward makeup with my index finger and squeezed my belly fat one last time before tearing myself away. I felt numb, then I felt sad. Lennie and my other housemates had already gone. All that was left to do was to leave the key on the kitchen counter, put on a hoodie, holster myself with the last couple of overstuffed bags of my belongings, slither down the dimly lit stairs, and kick open the door.

Outside, the sky was an anemic gray color and as I drove away I seemed to feel every pothole and bump in the road more acutely than before. I started to cry, feeling that this was definite confirmation that I was not, in fact, a sociopath. I remember driving on a very flat Ohio road, surrounded by very flat Ohio fields.

I've seen pictures of rice paddies and tiered gardens so colorful they resemble a Cosby sweater. Ohio's fields are the Cosby sweater's minimalist cousin who dropped out of art school because people there weren't "real" enough. Just like that cousin at a family reunion, people regularly in contact with Ohio terrain feel love for it at the same time that they harbor an inextinguishable hatred for it.

Across the fields was a geometric line of clouds producing a much more vigorous rainfall than the uncommitted drizzle currently causing my windshield wipers to squeak. I remember scoffing at it, this perfect symbolism. Like something out of a high school English teacher's wet dream, there it was: a linear reminder that that day so ultimately separated the past and the future. I crossed a couple county lines, the highway changed from two lanes to four, and exit signs started to display not one, but perhaps even four fast food placards. Stripped of former industrial prowess, prosperity in these places could now be measured in the number of choice in retailers whose product will clog arteries with the least amount of effort. Dying a few years younger is perfectly palatable if it tastes like bacon cheeseburgers. Don't try to understand if you're not from the heartland. If things here always made sense, the name of my hometown, Ravine, wouldn't be pronounced Ray-vonn, and I would have taken the exit that meant two less traffic lights before home. But driving through Plodis, the city to which Ravine is a suburb, was never an uplifting activity. On that day, I did not want to see ragged teddy bears stapled to utility poles as makeshift memorials, or the police expelling homeless people from the bike path beside the river. It would have upset me. That day, there was something vaguely comforting about the chemically-treated lawns and spandex-clad young mothers pushing jogging strollers in front of them. Amid so much change, my usual disdain for their impossibly skinny thighs and well-dressed infants was replaced with something reminiscent of warmth.

My parents' house had been built by a scholar—or perhaps only a dilettante in—Georgian architecture, and so we had a spacious porch with a strange laminate pebble floor covering I can only imagine my mother having picked from a catalog in the early nineties. I like to think it had been some half-rotten wooden slats beforehand, thereafter replaced by something undeniably plastic and durable. The ceiling, wooden slats preserved in large part by the countless coats of exterior paint that had been shellacked on to than over the years, was, at that time, the color of oatmeal. Most Georgian of all were the great pillars at the front of the porch. The day I came home, none of those details made an impression on me. I remember lumbering to my front door, my mother's manic smile bobbing as she appeared in the window. With considerable aplomb, she jerked the door open, and chirped at me.

"Hi, Sweetheart! How does it feel?"

"How does what feel?" I said.

"Being a college graduate, silly girl."

I shrugged my shoulders, but she would not be dismissed and words kept streaming from her mouth as she hugged me.

"Did you go out last night? Was it fun? Did people cry? Your father's watching *Cool Hand Luke*. Bob! Addie's home."

"Hi Addie," Dad yelled from the family room, unwilling or

unable to vacate his recliner for my homecoming.

"Yeah," I said, "I actually don't feel very good. I think I'll go lie down."

"Honey, we should really unpack your car. If it doesn't happen now, you're just going to leave it for a week and things will start to smell." Her eyes were wide, her mouth pursed into an encouraging, maternal half-smile.

I remember promising to unpack later and pretending not to hear her sigh as I trudged up the stairs. Nobody had died, and I wasn't being deprived of anything necessary for survival. I guess I should have found that comforting, but I didn't. All I could do, hungover and exhausted, was to face-plant on my bed, close my eyes, and enter a dead sleep so thorough I didn't even dream.

When I was very young, tucked between crisp white bed-sheets, I dreamt that my church had installed a soft-serve ice cream machine right in front of the pulpit. It may very well have been nothing more than a subconscious reaction to my mother's month-long ban of refined sugar in the house. Years later, however, that dream still represented a specific feeling, a combination of spiritual and physical sustenance that I had never been able to experience awake. I felt similarly lost after college, maybe because I was in the same room, surrounded by the same pale pink plaster walls covered with prints of pastoral country landscapes. Flanked by a bookshelf of awful juvenile fiction and a dresser covered with family photos, I woke later to the sight of my ancient clock radio. Were the dreams I had had so many years ago any closer to being fulfilled now that there was a college diploma on my vanity? At college, I'd been taught that most things left ample room for subjective interpretation, that I could mold thoughts, just like I imagined my sleeping brain to mold dreams, into the shape of whatever I needed them to be, even if that wasn't real. Now, the self I had created over the past four years mattered most to a specific set of inspectors who had been made irrelevant in the course of one ceremony. The things I had learned felt a bit like those tags on mattresses; objects that were of utmost importance in the factory but were promptly ripped off and discarded once home. College seemed a convergence of feelings that I'd always want to return to, but that would also be difficult to revisit.

I soon discovered that my tears on the car ride home might have been justified after all, though not for the reasons I had thought. Home was supposed to provide a comfortable nook to regress in. At twenty-two, I wasn't expecting to be rocked to sleep with lullabies and a glass of warm milk. However, I was not prepared for the fact that my mother's childhood cookery of dinners like beef stew and meatloaf had given way, almost exclusively, to pureed vegetable soups. The chilled cans of pop and homemade cookies had been replaced by fermented teas and gluten-free graham crackers whose number one ingredient was pea starch. The knowledge that I no longer had a curfew or was ultimately in charge of my own destiny was little comfort. Home, once a familiar protective barrier, began to feel like the very thing that was causing a surgical separation from the rest of the world. The bucolic scenes depicted on my bedroom walls, once a promise of future adventure, now seemed a mockery of my circumstances. I still looked sort of human, I could manipulate my mouth into shapes and produce something like speech. But I was unable, at some deep and basic level, to connect with those around me, to be one of them, to be back in a family.

At school, my "family" had consisted of Lennie and our other friends. We had bonded over shots of cheap booze, our drunkenness a common history made of equal parts belonging and bad decisions. Returning to a family of matronly concern and fiber-rich snacks no longer rang true as it had once done. I was constantly on edge. Any interaction with my parents was potentially the one to make me lose my shit, and with it my welcome into the fold of responsible adulthood. I've never read Frankenstein; but that's how I imagine myself then.

Years ago, after the ice cream dream, my mother had woken me with promises of a hot shower and breakfast, as though even she knew that reality would have to be a bit better dressed from then on. That May, I tried to convince myself that this life, with mother's free and heart-healthy red wine and my vibrator, might not be terrible after all. Instead, I found myself wondering how much wine I could filch before Mom would suggest Alcoholics Anonymous, or how I would explain the burn marks on my sheets when the vibrator, cheap as it was, inevitably overheated and caught fire.

College had always been sold to me as this magical fetus that would, upon graduation, be birthed and heralded as the second coming of Christ. I'd struggled through the labor pains (no epidural) and now I didn't have a fucking baby. I had a weird, benign tumor. Of course, I was supposed to be relieved and thankful. I was supposed to have a new lease on life. But whatever drugs they had given me to survive this ordeal weren't wearing off quite how they were supposed to.

A few days into my stupor, my mother, whose tolerability and level of progressivism were—as they are now—proportional to the amount of coffee she's consumed, appeared one morning at the doorway of the family room, where I had spent the night watching television and texting Lennie as Mom and Dad slept. Blessed with milky porcelain skin in her youth, her cheeks and nose now bore faint touches of rosacea, and her blue eyes, huge and round, recessed quite deeply into her skull. Her nose and chin turned upward, a snobby look at odds with her pilled fleece bathrobe. Her mop of curly brown hair was completely askew because of the REM Behavior Disorder that caused her to physically act out dreams. That was another detail I had conveniently repressed before hearing her claw at my bedroom door a few days earlier, muttering something about how the dog needed to be let out. Squinted eyes not yet adjusted to the light, she said:

"What on earth are you doing up?"

"Watching TV," I replied, as though the answer wasn't obvious.

"Well go to bed. *Living Blood* is on at 6:00, and I'll be watching it."

"What is *Living Blood*? How many vampire shows do we need?"

"It's a church program, Addie, about Jesus Christ. Go get some sleep."

There were circumstances in which I could have gotten some flexibility out of her. Those circumstances would never have included televangelism.

I hope that, just because I said I was from Ohio, referenced the regional penchant for processed food, and that my mother loves Jesus, my people have not become a caricatured collection of slack-jawed simpletons wandering through a corn maze. We may not be Manhattan, but old money can be found in the most straightforward of places, and that's what people actually mean when they say words like cosmopolitan and sophisticated. My grandparents, and their house, were a prime example of the industry that once blessed the Middle West. It was large, geometric, white stone, surrounded by violent-looking iron fencing, expanses of grass and forest, and well-tended flower beds. An outsider might have thought the house too aristocratic for its location, especially if they had driven past the freeway-adjacent purveyor of farm equipment on their way into Plodis. An outsider would soon be enlightened as to the differences between Ravine and Plodis. There weren't any fortified walls between the two, but Ravine had declared itself immune to the pitiful urban sprawl reserved for normal folk. Houses like Gran and Pop's were never particularly practical, but were a source of pride simply because they still stood on their own. No one had sold off lots in Ravine so that some horrible family living in a new four bedroom with aluminum siding could peer into their neighbors' windows.

When assholes from New York City or Los Angeles asked if I owned a tractor or enjoyed Nascar, I pictured the house, smiled smugly, and explained that I lived in a city. Superiority was always something I hated about Ravine, but I did not hesitate to visit it upon rude out-of-towners. The things we hate most when used against us are oddly comforting when we are finally granted the chance to wield them. If I then happened to remember the *Town and Country* article written about us, titled "Stock Prices Got You Down? Do as the Midwesterners Do and Invest in Family," I entered a second wave of self-loathing. Mother once let slip that Gran had never done Sunday dinners before that article, before the reporter had made a big thing of traveling from the East Coast to see how the "other half" lived. Much like the cultural institution that is *Town and Country* magazine, I assumed that the weekly Sunday dinners at Gran's had been borne of something like good intentions, something vaguely comforting. The necessity of both would always be nebulous, but both were traditions that wouldn't be ignored.

Gran didn't actually like to cook, and so, while food was given its last heating in the house's kitchen, its initial provenance was always mysterious, much like a tray lunch from the school cafeteria. That first Sunday back, just like always, I found her and her long, manicured fingernails gripping a foil take-out container of green beans, and pushing its contents into a china serving dish.

"Welcome home," she sighed, "Listen, will you put those pre-baked rolls in the oven?"

I did. She stared blankly out the window over the sink while nursing a glass of wine. One by one, family began trickling in. Every relative who lived in Ravine was required to come: my parents, me, my brother Palmer and his family, and my father's sister Kaye and her family. At the first Sunday dinner, people had probably milled about talking and joking. Years away from its inception, everyone arriving made a beeline for the dining room table, grabbing a drink beforehand to take the edge off. Once everyone was seated around the dining room table, Pop—a wizened but sharp character with a greying combover—said a prayer. His short-sleeved Oxford shirt folded in on itself as he clasped his hands tightly over his plate and his head tilted forward at such an angle that his bald spot was just visible. He would say the same thing each time, always in one breath as though he'd had to memorize it and wanted to get it all out before the last bit slipped his mind.

"Dear God. Thank you for the food we are about to receive and bless all those less fortunate. Amen."

Around the table were slight variations of the same posture, punctuated here and there by a glassy-eyed stare (Aunt Kaye), a clenched jaw (Dad), a really interesting bit of dirt underneath a fingernail (Uncle George), an insincere smile (Mother), and the quick reflexes needed to prevent one child from stabbing another with the family silver (my brother Palmer and his wife Nancy). Conversation followed a familiar pattern, with devout participation limited to just a few diners and half-hearted interjections from the rest of us. We had always followed a strict one-speaker-at-a-time policy, such that the sound of silverware scraping across china reminds me of family almost more than their actual voices. No exceptions were made. Even cousin Darwin, Kaye and George's child, and Nancy and Palmer's older kids knew to keep quiet. Pop and Dad always had a solid rotation of political statements, stock prices, and sports statistics to discuss, and maybe an article or two from the bowels of the *Plodis Daily News*. There were other rules of play. Dinners were also usually graced by wise pronounce-ments from Gran, prompted by the multiple glasses of Pinot Grigio she had drunk, and my mother laughing loudly at something that wasn't supposed to be funny. In fact, that dinner only stands out in my mind because I was expected to contribute to an uncom-fortably large portion of the conversation, being the one with the most future to figure out and all. It began after Gran called a rising star of local politics, and close business associate of my father's, a "poop." Awkward silence ensued, and Aunt Kaye swooped in, attempting to revive what Gran had just hit with a verbal kill shot.

"So, Addie, tell us: what are your plans now that you've graduated?"

Normally I liked Aunt Kaye. My father's sister, she was younger and a little edgy. She wore her hair in an un-suburban platinum bob, favored black clothes, and wasn't afraid to mix black nail polish with her glistening traditional engagement ring. I felt like we had an understanding that neither of us ever really wanted to be where we were. No matter how good-natured the asker of that question, however, I hated them almost as much as I hated having to tell Gran I'd voted Republican each time an elec-tion rolled around.

"Oh, you know, just working on the résumé, applying for jobs, writing cover letters. You know the drill."

"Yes, your mother said something about the United Nations.

I know you majored in Political Science, but what would you want to do there?"

"Well, I mean, I just wrote a thesis on the politics of revolution and regime change, so if I could get something that in some way relates to that, that would be nice."

"The U.N. has a fun international vibe. Would you ever be interested in living abroad?"

"I think so, for a few years."

Gran started with one of her monologues on the merits of early marriage, or how she'd never want to live anywhere foreign. Kaye let her finish, then resumed talking.

"You know, George was in South America years ago for research, right, honey?"

"Yes," her husband George replied, evidently a little annoyed at being nudged into speaking, "Chilé."

"Really?" I asked, "What were you doing there?"

"It was when I was working for the Pharmaceutical Company. I spent a few months taking plant specimens in the rainforest there."

"I'd love to go to Easter Island someday," I replied, clarifying for my mother's benefit,

"It's off the coast of Chilé."

Gran interrupted again, opining that she found the "head statues" creepy. George chastised her for not calling them *moai*; his intellectual anguish would not have allowed otherwise.

"That's a nice jacket, George," Gran rebutted, "Where'd you get it? A rummage sale?"

The back-and-forth continued for another hour or so, while people ate bites of turkey with gravy that had the consistency of hot fudge and had left a brown stain on the glass jar it had been poured out of. There was dry stuffing and bagged salad that had been served with about eight dressing options, all of which were fat free. Gran had bought a pie from the chic new bakery on Main Street, whose name she didn't understand ("Who calls a bakery 'The Sweet Tooth'? People aren't going to eat sugar if they're thinking of their dental bills.") She offered dessert to everyone, though she only meant for the men to accept. Every female in the family had been told at least once to "reduce," and peppered with helpful advice to accomplish the same. *Use lettuce instead of bread when you make sandwiches. Low-sodium broth will keep you from passing out. Never buy any dairy that hasn't had all of the fat removed from it.* I ate the pie, as I always did, with ice cream, ignoring Gran's dirty looks and backhanded comments about finding a husband or "missing out on life." An hour later I was back on the couch at home, watching shitty television, drinking an annoyingly moderate quantity of wine, and commiserating via phone with Lennie about our perceived reversal of fortunes.

A sort of post-graduate momentum would arrive the following Wednesday in the person of Eduardo Soares. Leaving college had eroded most of my conception of time or normalcy, but even I knew that something untoward was happening when my mother's high-pitched cackle traveled up to my bedroom from the patio out back, and the door to my father's den closed a minute later. I had lived away from home long enough to forget the unlikely phenomenon of Mom hosting resident artists in our pool house (basically a decorated garage, called the pool house only in reference to the tiny lap pool my father had installed for his fiftieth birthday). A week after I left for college, a graffiti artist from Britain had come, chain-smoking clove cigarettes and sneaking out at all hours to spray paint thought-provoking social messages on the industrial sarcophagi in Plodis. Apparently another one had been summoned to celebrate my homecoming. As my father's hasty retreat into the den would suggest, the rest of us tended to cope with these invasions by hiding and pretending that everything was normal.

None of us knew how Mom had found out about this opportunity or why she had decided to go through with it. She was notorious for having involved conversations with strangers in grocery stores and post offices, and returning home with "great" ideas. Our family had outsiders to thank for such experiments as giving panhandlers raw, vegan meal-replacement bars instead of spare change. The house had nearly been set on fire once when she decided to start a home candy-making business. I could only assume that a stranger's wisdom was also the impetus for the creative folk in the pool house.

This idea would never have occurred to my father, and I think he tolerated the disruption as penance for his job-related absence during our childhoods. He was equally complicit in the hushing of whatever protests the rest of the family raised. If having "artists" in the garage would allow him to read the newspaper and drink scotch in peace, he would tolerate it.

Sufficiently wrested from my slumber, I went to the kitchen and poured some cereal, covertly stealing glances at the invasive bohemian seated on the patio. He was a spindly wisp of a man, darkly complected and dressed for some sort of homeless social experiment. Dark socks, leather clogs, skintight corduroy pants, a ratty striped oxford, a wool sweater with several conspicuous holes. He had a scrubby black beard and shoulder-length straight hair of the same color that had been angrily pulled into a rabbit's foot of a ponytail. Mother came in from the patio.

"Addie, you should introduce yourself to Eduardo..." she paused after actually seeing me, "...when you've changed into something more app-rop-pri-ate."

"I didn't realize we were having another artist," I said.

"I'm sure I mentioned it to you at some point."

She hadn't, but I moved on.

"What's he do?"

"Oh, it's all very interesting. He's from Argentina, or maybe Portugal, I can't remember which. Anyway, folk musician. He's going to compose a symphony entirely out of sounds he records around the city. He said the first few measures are just going to be cars turning on and off. Cool, huh?"

"Why's he being a chode and sitting by himself?"

"Addie, if I have to look at your nipples, I won't tolerate you using that word. He just finished a cigarillo. All he wanted to drink was coffee."

"A, I have a shirt on, B, have you seen pictures of yourself in the 1970s? And C, in all of Ravine High School, I don't think I ever saw anyone looking so anorexic or needy."

"Oh, stop it. He's an artist. He's allowed to be a little odd. And just because you're jealous of his metabolism doesn't mean you can be rude."

I ignored the subtle dig at my weight. She would say she hadn't meant anything by it anyway.

"Maybe he's odd," I said, "or maybe he's a giant douchebag."

"You give him a chance, and watch your damn mouth. And, Addie, please just go put on a bra."

As she often did at the end of a litany of commands, she descended into the basement to sort laundry. Or watch *Living Blood*. In those days, it was hard to tell. When she returned to find me still in the kitchen, and without bra, something snapped. Perhaps visions of forty-year-old me, still braless, fat, unemployed and sitting on her couch were swirling in her head. Before I knew it, I was appeasing her by telling her that I was going to go to the library to work on job applications, though I had no intention of doing anything of the sort. I called Lennie, hoping for some wise counsel.

"Hey, girl, hey," she warbled throatily.

"Hi," I whined, "I miss Darden so much. Can we go back, please?"

"Would love. I would give my left arm for a Long Island from the bar right now."

"Why the left arm?"

"Because I'm not ambidextrous, silly goose. I couldn't just start signing my name with my left hand. How's home?"

"Sucks. I'm walking to the library right now because my mother won't stop bitching at me about a job. How's home?"

"Meh. I mean, my mom is getting me some bullshit job at Purge's corporate office. A, I haven't shopped there since middle school when I thought looking slutty was cool, and B, they have the worst human resources practices known to man. My cousin worked there and gained like twenty pounds after a really bad break-up and they fired her for being too fat. I hope they don't expect me to use lunch breaks to go to the gym. I'd die."

"Well, it's only for a while, right?"

"Yeah, I guess. I mean, at least I'll be making some money."

"Maybe it will suck less if you think about it from a sociological standpoint." I said. Sociology had been her major.

"At least you'll have something to do."

The Ravine Public Library is on the town square, which, shockingly, is a square of grass with a gazebo in the middle. I suppose once upon a time it was a pristine expanse of uniform sod. Now, awkward patches of different greens where chemicals had been applied to make up for foot traffic were scattered throughout. The library is a stately box of a building, made of stone the color of a dirty band-aid, graced with beautiful wrought-iron accents and big picture windows. The steps leading to the main entrance are inexplicably made of sandstone, such that tracks inevitably appear where all of the library patrons have trod on them. Given my limited cognitive function that day, I headed straight for the audio-visual department to look for movies. Nestled in a corner of the basement, there were seemingly endless hunter green steel shelves brimming with cinematic selections. The movies, in their clear plastic cases, were arranged in alphabetical order, and I always browsed from A-Z. *All About Eve, Beaches*; my eyes scanned feverishly over the rows, finding comfort in their organization, their uniformity. *East of Eden, French Kiss...*

"Hey Addie."

I turned to find myself face to face with Tyler Hogue, a high school classmate. During my adolescence, I had avoided any place of business with Ravine in the title (Ravine Public Library, Ravine Savings Bank, Ravine Community Pool) because chances were good I'd run into someone I knew there, and God knows I didn't want that. I guess I had stopped caring: repeated alcohol consumption and fuzzy-headed lack of direction will do that for you.

"Oh, hey," I replied reflexively, "How are you?"

"Just, you know, living with my parents, trying to find a job. You?"

"Same. Where did you go to school again?" I knew that he went to an Ivy, but I pretended to know nothing about him, just like I always had.

"Yale. Finance. You?"

"Darden. Political Science."

"Darden. There were a lot of people from our class who

went there, right?"

"A few, yeah. I never really saw them, though, except for at the bar sometimes."

"Right. Well, I'll let you get back to your browsing, but we should hang out sometime and catch up."

"Sure," I replied cheerfully, more focused on the fact that the interaction was nearing its close than on the faint implication of future social engagement.

As I walked home, thoughts raced through my brain. I thought that my social anxiety was gone, but evidently Ravine stirred it right back up.

Hang out? Catch up? We weren't even friends in high school. What the hell is there to catch up on? Did I just have a functional encounter with someone from my high school? Someone popular? I mean, popular in the sense that his parents had a stocked liquor cabinet and went out of town a lot. But seriously, what the fuck just happened? Do things change just like that? One second I hate you because I can't get through second-period math without hearing about who fucked who last weekend at your tawdry house party, and the next we're chatting in the library, and we have fancy degrees, and need to "catch up"? Was that at all sincere? Probably just being polite, right? I'm not going to hear from him ever again. Jesus, Addie, chill the fuck out.

In the days that followed, it became very clear very quickly that if I wanted to avoid the smoke of Eduardo's cigarillos, I would need to stay as far away from the patio as possible. Given my lack-luster first impression of him and my propensity for binge-watch-ing television, keeping to myself wasn't very difficult. I hadn't automatically ruled out being sociable, but at every turn another reason seemed to appear for me to keep to myself. If the nearly endless stench of Black and Milds wasn't enough, I had stood by an open window on the stairs one day to hear him consoling my mother for her underdeveloped artistic skills. Since I was a child, she's been telling the same story to anyone who will listen about her ruined ambition. In Ohio, people generally listen to another person talk politely until they absolutely cannot handle it anymore, so she'd had plenty of practice perfecting her spiel. Through the window screen, I heard Eduardo's question, and I knew exactly where it would lead.

"What about you Joan, do you make art?" he lilted, thick with accent, "I always say you cannot be a supporter of the arts without first having the soul of an artist."

Barf.

"Well, you know, I used to paint," replied my mother, "I took a parks and rec class years and years ago before I had Palmer. The teacher told me I had real talent, you know. But, I couldn't stay up all night painting when I had a baby to tend to."

"You could start again," Eduardo suggested.

I didn't stay to listen to the rest. I could hear it in my head, the dialogue that would ensue, that *had* ensued at holiday meals and neighborhood block parties and with retail clerks and hair-dressers. She wouldn't try again to paint. She would "leave that up to the real artists." It really pissed me off, this attitude that she was close enough to death to give up on a passion. It couldn't be as fulfilling to selectively nurture the ambitions of others. Furthermore, she always told the story as though the babies had been forced upon her, some imposing presence. I knew my women's history. The pill existed well before my brother did. Perhaps because in my role as her child, I was a disrupter of her interests, I was never accorded the same encouragement to follow my passion. I had taken art classes in high school and she was never enthusiastic about my self-portraits and still-lifes. The title "artist" enchanted her. Evidently her children reminded her, with a thud, that she was not an artist, but a mom. The thought of trying to be both was out of the question. There was laundry to sort.

I tried not to make the resentment mutual. I read *The Feminine Mystique* in the eighth grade. I understand that women need more than vacuum cleaners and babies for fulfillment. What bothered me more was the fact that she couldn't separate me and my brothers from the artistic dreams she had drowned. We were the cement shoes weighing down the life she might have had. Eduardo, and all those like him, I guess, gave her a chance to talk to the dead, if only for a fleeting moment.

Each in our own way, the entire family vacillated between grandiosity and depression. We all suffered from a unique brand of self-involvement, rotationally becoming indignant when attention fell to anyone else. None of us would have known what to do if all of our emotional needs had suddenly been met. Looking back, that seems a hallowed Midwestern fable; search for identity in a homogenous land. Life was trying to set oneself apart amid miles of genetically identical corn stalks, and retreating into the same when individuality became too painful.

I hadn't unpacked yet. I could tell my mother wanted me to, if not by the way she would pull my bedroom door closed every time she walked past, than by the post-it notes she left on top of my heap of belongings night after night "reminding" me to do so. Housework bored me. When I was a child, and still on my weakest-willed of days, I imagined what life would look like when I had arrived, when I was happy and wanted for nothing. As an eight-year-old, I saw my future self as a female Daddy Warbucks, in a great marble mansion brimming with servants and unmitigated wealth, where everything was clean and I never *had* to do anything. I would have lots of daughters so that I could dress them in matching, fashionable outfits and give each of them not one, but two extravagant-sounding middle names. At eighteen, I thought about my dream man: a tall, dark, and handsome attorney who specialized in civil rights cases or something supporting a just cause. He would share my liberal beliefs, but also have some family money to fall back on, because we would both acknowledge that idealism wasn't lucrative. We would be bound by the understanding that we wanted to enjoy our enlightened view of the world through a picture window regularly cleaned by a third party.

Both of those dreams had been shredded in the depressing reality of my post-collegiate life, but I still wasn't motivated to clean. My back supported by my bed frame, I was hemmed in by memories. A giant tupperware container of clothes that had only been bought for the purpose of wearing to theme parties (I don't know why I kept the coconut bra. I just couldn't let it go), a basket of cheap picture frames adorned with glitter and puffy paint, a stack of outdated textbooks, and a month's supply of underwear. My laptop screen was open to the *Huffington Post*, where I could learn about recent political developments *and* judge for myself the severity of the latest side-boob debacle. Though I no longer really wanted to be Daddy Warbucks, and had resigned myself to the improbability of finding a handsome, rich, and idealistic man, distracting myself in the blue glow of my computer screen seemed much more palatable than cramming adult-sized clothes into my child-sized dresser.

Some period of time later, my vibrating phone woke me. Carpet pattern imprinted on my cheek, I called Lennie back as I went to the kitchen in search of some wine.

"Hey, girl! How's the job search going?"

"It's not."

"Something will come along. I ran into your mother today."

"Really? Where?"

"The mall. I want to hear about this latin lover in the pool house. Has he serenaded you yet?"

"I haven't even formally met him yet, and honestly, his music is probably awful."

"Who cares about his music? At least you'll have something to do. Is he cute?"

"Kind of a greasy hipster type."

"Well, where does he fall on the FMD?"

Lennie was referring to the overly simplistic rating system we had used throughout college almost exclusively on people we never had social contact with to determine whether they were fuckable, marriageable, or dateable. Rather crass, and based more on TV shows than our own lives, it stayed not because it was accurate, but because we all thought ourselves clever for having made the taxonomy. Basically, the fuckable label applied to all those we'd theoretically drunkenly ravage if given the chance. Being marriageable meant that they'd probably be tolerable past the sex, maybe even to the point of cooking breakfast. Extra points were awarded in this category for things like: he's a really good big brother, or he volunteers at an animal shelter. Dateable men were those who were great company for cuddling and watching a movie, and they'd probably pay for your dinner, and open doors and things. Despite their niceness, however, you kind of always felt like you'd ditch them at a moment's notice for a night out with your girlfriends.

"He's not on the scale," I replied, pausing for a generous swill of Merlot.

"Addie, he's a musician. He has to be on the scale. Stop being so picky."

"He's not on the scale. I did run into this guy at the library, though."

"Of course you did. FMD?"

"Maybe all of them if I weren't reliving my adolescent trauma. He went to fucking Yale."

"Oh my God! You have to hang out with him."

My mother found me the next morning watching a documentary about Woodstock. I hadn't slept. I had just gotten to the point where they were interviewing the guys who emptied out the port-a-johns. Even with all of their free love and idealism in the air, everybody was still full of shit. The coffee pot, on a timer, began to seize and spit every morning at five-thirty, perhaps in anticipation of the televangelism it was about to witness. I could have used this as an alarm of sorts, to avoid early-morning confrontation, but my lethargy didn't allow for that. Her initial, pre-coffee salvo consisted of old favorites like:

"Why are you still awake?"

"How are you ever going to be able to work a normal job, the hours you keep?"

"What trash are you watching?"

That morning, she disappeared to get her coffee, sure to return with more heartening counsel. Only this morning, she returned not with a coffee cup, but with the wine bottle I'd drained the previous evening.

"Do I need to be worried about this?" she asked, "Because I really don't have time for this crap."

"What?" I said, "I rinsed it and put it in the recycling."

"Adelaide, you know what I mean. I've had it. Get some sleep, then wake up and find a job. I can't do this with you all summer."

"You realize I've only been here for like two weeks, right?"

"You're going to have to take some initiative soon, you know. You're never going to be able to move out if you sit around in your pajamas all the time and never shampoo your hair."

"I'll live in the pool house," I said.

"You can't live in the pool house, Addie. Eduardo is living in the pool house."

"So, you'll subsidize a shiftless artist whose music doesn't sound like music, but your own daughter can't watch a little TV after frying her brain for four years?"

"Don't give me that bad parent crap, Addie. Your father and I paid a quarter of a million dollars for your brain frying. You know, at your age, I already had Palmer, and your father was in business school. We never moved back home."

"Jesus, you act like Women's Lib never happened. No one forced you to have Palmer. The reason you never moved back home was because you were married and the economy wasn't complete shit."

"Don't take the name of the Lord in vain!" She glared at me. "Go to bed."

I went back to the library to get more movies. I told myself I didn't care whether I ran into Tyler Hogue again, but my application of mascara and choice of a flowered dress said differently. I had a habit, in those days, of blindly supposing that if I trusted fate, it would bring me happiness. A sliver at a time, I would relinquish some control and predict the future. If I showed some leg and put on some lip gloss, I told myself, maybe I'd meet my true love and just know. When you met your true love, you just knew. My predictions never came true, and I'd get irrationally angry that destiny wasn't the exact same as what I supposed it would be, but it never took long for me to tempt fate again. I lingered this time as I pored over movie titles, leaving footprints in the lush red carpet from *Alfie* to *Zoolander*. I heard my name again.

"Addie! Welcome home!" said my mother's friend Katherine Holt.

I think most people found her a tad annoying, maybe even my mother. She had a loud, high-pitched voice, a tendency to cut others off both in speech and in traffic, and an addiction to spray-on tans that never quite looked right. She was too kind for anyone to outright reject, and had ingratiated herself into the social structure of Ravine well-enough to know something about everyone. She was a lawyer, I think, settling cases somewhere, always in some kind of suiting and on the phone.

"Oh, hi Katherine! Thank you. How are you doing?"

"Oh, pretty good, kiddo. This week has just been a nightmare. We're getting our roof re-done, slate, costing us an absolute fortune, and I've got this case that I need to wrap up before we head to the lake house, which I'm sure is just a mess since our cleaning lady moved. How are you?"

Immediately after asking me this question, her eyes became glued to her cell phone, never moving as I spoke, though she offered a few monosyllabic sounds to signal that she was, in fact, listening. She looked up.

"Did your mother tell you Meredith's engaged? You all were about the same age, right? Oh, here, let me find a picture of her and Logan," she chirped as she began spastically scrolling through photos on her phone. A few minutes later, after having been shown an engagement picture of her daughter, who hadn't even graduated yet, and whose diamond looked larger than the amount of food that she ate at a meal, I offered a congratulatory phrase and turned to go. Rather than walking up the stairs, though, I found myself making a beeline for the closest bathroom. Locked in a stall, I suddenly couldn't breathe. My hearing was muffled, as though I was submerged in water, and all I could seem to focus on was the amount of labor involved in each inhale and exhale. I sat on the toilet immobile for a few moments, unable to think or to move, in the throes of a panic attack for no apparent reason.

Fuck! Who is using a hammer in the library in middle of the day? It's not a hammer, you dumbass. It's the sound of your own heart beating in your ears. How long are you going to stare at the floor tiles? Get up. You don't need to look at yourself in the mirror. Walk upstairs. Walk home.

I got up, hearing still dominated by the fuzzy mallet I imagined on my bass drum heart. Eyes straight ahead, I left the library and watched my feet walking home as images flooded my brain. Slate roofs, blown-dry hair, engagement rings, manicured nails, fertilized lawns, and ornamental hedges filled me with anxiety. Cute mailboxes, in-ground sprinkler systems, intense joggers, cookouts, badminton, babies in cardigans, dogs with grosgrain ribbon around their necks made it hard to breathe. My eyes out of focus, I thought of Starbucks lattes, newly painted shutters, brick fireplaces, privacy fences, bleached teeth, and tennis courts and willed myself to walk faster till I reached home. I felt drunk, but not carefree as I slid down the back of my bedroom door, wishing that it locked and seeking solace by tracing the edges of the crown molding with my fingertips. None of it made sense, and I couldn't begin to explain it, and all I could do was crawl into my bed and make everything disappear by closing my eyes. The images being projected onto the back of my closed eyelids became less frenetic, my heart rate slowed, and—thoroughly exhausted by an everyday errand—I drifted into sleep.

I woke up later in complete darkness. I was still in my dress, mascara smeared. I felt silly as I turned on the sad overhead light and collected my movies from where I had half-consciously dropped them on the floor. I wanted not to feel anything at all. I found my mother in the kitchen, scouring the sink as she did every night before she went to bed. I went to get a glass of wine to ease my sorrows, but found no wine bottle in its usual space.

"Mom," I said, "Did you move the wine?"

"Yes," she replied.

"Are you gonna tell me where you put it?" I countered.

"No," she said.

"What?" I said, as she kept her back to me, scrubbing the sink. She turned around dramatically, be-gloved and holding a sponge in her hands like a microphone.

"I hid it," she said, "You shouldn't be drinking wine every

night. I'm concerned."

"You drink wine every night," I regurgitated.

"Addie, I'm an adult. I have a house. I'm stable. When you've gotten a job and aren't sleeping during the day, we can re-assess."

I slammed the cupboard closed and adjourned to the couch. A few minutes later, her cleaning ritual complete, she appeared in the doorway, clutching a mug and looking at me as though I had become a stripper and she was trying to figure out what she had done wrong.

"Oh, Addie, you know I only do this because I love you, right? I'm your number one fan."

"Mom," I replied, my eyes fixed on the TV, "You know who else says that? Kathy Bates in *Misery*. Are you going to hold me hostage in a country house and murder me?"

"I know it's hard for you to accept that I'm older and wiser than you, but that's the truth," she retorted, "And plan on coming to church with your father and I tomorrow. Maybe God can give you a sense of direction. You know He loves you more than I do."

"Goodnight, Mommie Dearest," I replied.

She hated when I called her this, even if she did share a first name with Joan Crawford. I thought about just staying in bed and ignoring her religious directive. When I still hadn't fallen asleep at 7:30 am, I resigned myself to putting on makeup and biting the bullet. Maybe if I was lucky it would be full of cyanide instead of gunpowder.

Worship, on the surface, has always been sold to me as something wholesome, comforting and traditional. It is constant. It never changes. Though organized religion is not exclusively Midwestern, it fits in well with football games and neighborhood picnics, plopped onto gingham tablecloths in between casseroles and macaroni salads. Much like a plate heaped with some mixture of butter, eggs, sour cream, cheese, meat, potatoes, and the occasional pseudo-vegetable (canned green beans and the like), religion has the potential to make life delicious. Unfortunately, both religion and casseroles often lead to some acid reflux in the short run, and with steady and continued consumption, can mean high blood pressure, or a heart attack, even an untimely death. Everyone who eats casseroles knows this, of course, but that doesn't stop them from taking seconds. The health implications of religion are less clear-cut. Though my mother's makeover of our pantry suggested that she understood the ill effects of saturated fat and cholesterol, she was perfectly happy to dole out hazardous amounts of tradition in other forms, including church attendance.

Properly attired, I wandered into the kitchen in search of caffeine to find both of my parents preparing for their weekly dose of Jesus. My mother was ironing a cardigan in the corner, while also sipping orange juice, downing her morning pills, and running her fingers through the oddly shaped hanks of hair her curling iron had left. I sat at the table, where my father was calmly reading the paper, having been completely ready for at least an hour.

"Shoot, we're going to be late," my mother shrieked, "Bob, go start the car so we can go to Starbucks before. Bob!"

Dad, tearing his eyes from his reading, murmured something vaguely affirmative before jingling his keys in his pocket and heading for the station wagon. I followed, both of us knowing that we would sit in a parked car for five minutes while my mother tore around the house, unplugging small appliances and gathering various and sundry items from at least three separate rooms in the house. This holding pattern repeated a few minutes later in the Starbucks parking lot.

"Aren't there always like eight tureens of coffee at church?" I asked.

"Your mother doesn't care for it," Dad replied as Mom climbed back into the front seat.

"Church coffee is crap," she said, "Only the pastor and cheap old ladies drink it. Oh my God! Bob, look, Betsy Johnson just ran into the Smith's car. I hope they make it into the sanctuary before the doors close."

I soon learned that not much had changed about church services at Ravine Church since I'd been a kid. There were lots of families who might just have walked off of a LIFE game board. There was always a kid playing a Gameboy through the entire service. Just as I remembered, my father looked like he would fall asleep during the sermon, and Mom mouthed the words to hymns as her eyes darted from side to side, sizing up the other parishioners. If Sunday had really been a day of rest (as the Bible proclaims) in Ravine, people wouldn't have been piling on the money in layers and getting into fender benders in the Starbucks parking lot. Maybe, though, that discrepancy was beside the point.

Later, we all trouped over to the house for family dinner. Gran poured me a glass of wine.

"How's that freak in the pool house doing?" she asked.

"I don't really know," I replied, "Mom talks to him much more than I do."

"Well, if you ever need a place to work without that racket as a distraction, you can come and use the library. Pop and I hardly ever go in there. There's a good old desk."

"Thanks," I replied, a bit thrown off by her niceness.

It wasn't the generosity of the offer that puzzled me. Gran would have cut off an arm to help any of us if she thought we needed it. The catch was that she was also unafraid to inflict metaphorical injury on others, and thus her love manifested differently. In the moments when she wasn't harsh out of concern for someone's own good, she was lovely. I just always expected for the other shoe to drop.

"You know, Janice Hogue says Tyler mentioned that he ran into you."

"Yes, that's right," I said. There it was. She thought I'd met a potential husband.

"He's very handsome," Gran continued, "Is he single?"

"I don't know," I said.

"Well, if I were you, I'd find out."

Thankfully, Nancy came to interrupt.

"Hey, Addie," she said, nursing a gin and tonic, "Are you

interested in watching the kids a few days a week? I definitely could get out of the house and you could use some cash until you find something more permanent."

"Yeah, sure," I said. That would keep Mom and Dad off my back for another couple of weeks, and she and Palmer always kept a stocked pantry.

My mother looked annoyed in the opposite corner of the room. Annoyed that Gran was throwing a wrench in her efforts to control my drinking, annoyed that she'd never quite been able to break into Gran's inner circle, sure that I was punishing her. Which I suppose I was, in a way. I would normally have felt guilty about the mere possibility of hurting her feelings, but I was trying not to feel at all.

JUNE

I remember when Palmer announced that he was going to propose to Nancy. It was at a Sunday dinner. I remember primarily because through all the congratulations and toasts and smiles, my mother's eyes never stopped twitching. It's not that she had anything against Nan, I don't think, or that she ever has. I think she more took issue with the idea of her, the uniformity of her, the fact that my mother couldn't imagine her without a pair of toile curtains in the background. For my mother to have expected anything besides this is curious, because she raised both of my brothers to be fairly robust model Ravinites. The typical male archetype in Ravine, or at least the one that tends to be most lauded, is the prosperous and well-suited young man, who excels first in athletics, and second in multiplying wealth. In his younger days, Palmer moved to the East Coast for college: Harvard. Could have been Princeton, or Yale, or the family favorite of Penn. The only people who differentiate between the Ivies are those who are educated at them. Nobody else knows the difference, or cares.

He studied economics, or mathematics, or actuarial science; something numerical and esoteric. That's where he met Nancy (I always called her Nan.)

Nan looked just like the popular girls I went to high school with: blond and spindly and perfectly preppy and polished. When they first got serious, Gran checked around to make sure Nan was from a "good family." Old money, parents with lucrative and respectable professions, and a childhood farmhouse with a meadow somewhere generic and colonial in New Jersey. Nan relocated to Ravine after the wedding. This was an act of ostensible subservience in Gran's eyes, and for that, there was a slim chance that Gran wouldn't demonize Nan as an outsider who couldn't be trusted and would ultimately ruin the family name the first time one of her children misbehaved. This had not been the case for my mother. Raised in affluent Kentucky by a father who was a Senator and a mother who was an Evangelical, Mom's country roots had never impressed Gran. Around the time Mom was in high school, her father was caught accepting bribes and sent to federal prison on racketeering charges. It wasn't long after that that she had gone to college and married my father. Her Dad's public incarceration hadn't gone over well with Gran. I wondered sometimes if Mom's life might have been different if her father hadn't broken any laws, whether she would have ended up in quite so safe and homogenous a place. I think she wondered too. When her mother-in-law still laughed derisively at the mention of Kentucky, Grandpa Ted, or Grandma Sue, how could she not wonder?

Anyway, I think Nan found the idea of marrying into wealth somewhere unknown romantic, if only in a simple oxford-and-boat-shoe kind of way. Nan and Ravine together made sense. The summer after she and Palmer graduated, and had a nice wedding at her parents' country club, she'd packed up her appropriately aged luxury SUV and driven happily to Ohio. Less than a year later, she'd given birth to their first son, and by the time I'd come home from college they had four kids. I have no idea what she studied in college, or whether she'd had aspirations for some sort of job before she started procreating. They lived in an old brick house that was painted over with a disgustingly neutral glossy, beige paint. The picture of Americana, they (Palmer, Nan, Alexander, Madeleine, Charlotte, Leo, and the dog, Dorian) had family portraits taken in front of the lilac bushes they'd planted in the backyard.

In many respects, they were just like other young families in Ravine, spitting forth new children to be molded and polished, to continue the rivalries with the private schools in Plodis, to add another coat of pride to the bubble that encases well-maintained sidewalks and laughably low crime rates. It paid well to become an accomplice in this enterprise, and the kids were sweet. Newly re-incorporated into the fold, I knocked on the beige door and went into the beige house that June. Inside, everything was clean and everything was beautiful. Though each accent had been belabored and chosen most carefully, each throw pillow or tchotchke was meant to look like a perfect afterthought.

Alexander, newly seven, was already seated at the kitchen island eating "natural" toaster waffles when I arrived, wearing madras shorts and a polo. His ruddy cheeks and mussed chestnut hair exemplified the very sort of aristocratic composition that I supposed Gran liked for the family to exude, his forays into competition well-documented in pictures stuck to the fridge.

"Hey, Aunt Addie," he said, "Do you know that Addie rhymes with Maddy?"

Madeleine stared at him blankly for a second before turning her attention to me and telling me she was five years old while holding up a five-fingered hand as proof. Her short bob, brown in winter, had begun to lighten from exposure to the sun, and, before long, Nan was carefully combing through it and pinning it back with an oversized bow. Charlotte, three, was running in circles around the ground floor of the house, clutching a doll with which she shared an alabaster, Victorian complexion, and cutting corners a bit too closely. Last but not least was Leo, just over a year, who had been sitting quietly in his high chair, pushing Cheerios around on the tray in front of him, and occasionally looking up when things got especially loud. He looked like all the rest of them; together they appeared the perfect corn-fed family: the picture of Midwestern tradition. All they needed was a baseball and an apple pie and they'd look like a Norman Rockwell drawing.

Though not in charge of an efficient and lucrative business, Nan's daily life had the precise scheduling maintained by a CEO. That day was Monday, for example, which meant several things must happen. She had an appointment with her personal trainer, a garishly tan middle-aged woman named Cher who looked perpetually burnt to a crisp but got "results" for women who were already thin and toned. Nan would also do some errands. She'd been waffling about a scarf she bought in Plodis and had decided at last to return it. Lunch at the club with a friend, the dry cleaning, and an artisanal butcher for the week's meat were also on the list.

"Addie," she said flusteredly as she darted out the door in a sporty tank and leggings, gym tote slung over her arm, highlighted hair pulled into a glossy ponytail, "Alex and Maddy have to be at camp at the park at nine, and then you can drop off Charlotte at her playgroup right after that. She'll get picked up at noon, and then I'll grab the other two from camp on my way home from the butcher around three."

"Okay," I said, "Sounds good."

Hardly taking a breath, she continued, "The keys to the van are hanging on the third hook next to the back door. Palmer took his Porsche to the office so I can drive the Beemer and leave you the van, alright?"

The screen door slammed and she was gone. It could have been because I had not had coffee yet that morning, but the four children energetically swirling around me made me feel as though their house, in spite of its neutral, overstuffed sofas and wealth of pretty organizational containers from an overpriced home goods store, was chaos itself.

"Alright," I said, "Does everyone have their shoes on?"

Like a Greek chorus, they responded all at once, "No. No. No." Of course their little shoes were all in a row in a spotless mudroom. After corralling them into the van, which contained two different booster seats, a car seat, and dvd screens strapped onto the backs of the seats, we set off on our journey. City Park, where the Ravine Parks Bureau holds its yearly summer camp, was just a couple of blocks away, and we could have walked, but nobody ever did. I had to drive several laps around the parking lot just to find a space, then unload all of them for the fifty-yard walk to the pavilion used for signing in. Their friends were there and instant connections were made over matching superhero shoes and an impromptu game of tag. Such unfettered enthusiasm for life reminded me of the seemingly carefree place I had just left and for a moment I wanted to be drunk, with Lennie, expressing opinions about things that didn't matter, rather than shaping America's youth. I dropped Charlotte off at the community center to a room full of tired toddlers, and then I had just a little bit of time where my only concern was Leo. Leo was quieter than the others. He sat on laps, he listened to stories, and, I thought, he appeared to prefer adjectives to verbs. With the dappled sun shining through the curtains onto a very specific patch of off-white carpet, the most complicated thing in front of me was building a block tower for him to knock down. Life seemed tolerable. The phone rang; it was Nan.

"Hey Addie, listen, I just got out of the shower at the gym, and the salon has a cancellation, and my highlights are so grown out I feel like a strung-out model, so I'm going to go and get my hair colored, too, if that's okay with you."

I could hardly refuse her. I had nothing else to do with my time, other than sleep, and besides, it was another ten dollars in my pocket.

"Okay," I said.

"So, Alex and Maddy get picked up from camp at 2:30, okay?"

"Sure."

The afternoon contained another list of seemingly endless tasks. Change the diaper, refill the sippy cup, gather toys for the car, make sure the diaper bag is stocked just in case disaster strikes, lock the house, unlock the car, strap Leo into his carseat, buckle myself in and take a deep breath before I back out of the drive. Pick up Charlotte at the community center, load them both back into the car, hurry home for lunch. Cut up tiny bites of deli meat, get out crackers, get out baby carrots, cut grapes in half, pour the right kind of juice into the right kind of cup. Listen to Charlotte as she tells me about herself. Her favorite color is pink. Her best friend at playgroup, Lily, is going to the beach this week. She has a doll named Winnie. She can do a somersault. Soon she'll start swim lessons, and Mommy will take her to buy a new swimsuit. Her one-sided banter continued unabated through her peanut butter and jelly, which I suppose made my life easier. I didn't have to come up with questions like "If you had to choose between Cinderella and Ariel, who would win?" I put on some ridiculous TV show featuring household objects brought to life with copious amounts of googly eyes for her and Leo. They sat on the couch placidly staring at the screen and clutching blankies while I cleaned up after lunch. Sitting with them, I tried not to fall asleep before it was once again time to rally the troops and pick up the remaining siblings.

In my sleep-deprived and unenthusiastic state, I had chosen an outfit that seemed reasonable for the care of small children: yoga pants, an obnoxiously brightly colored sorority t-shirt, and flip-flops. Silly me. I wasn't in college anymore. I was in Ravine. One of Nan's ilk approached me, uniform complete: her red hair perfectly straight, flawless make-up, a light-pink polo shirt, khaki bermuda shorts and Jack Rogers sandals, manicured nails, diamond ring, the whole nine yards. Though she was perilously close to invading my personal space, she didn't address me.

"Hi Leo," she crowed, "Don't you look adorable today," an aside: "Leo's mommy and I play tennis together."

Gratifyingly, Leo turned his face from her. She clearly thought I was just another babysitter, not to be bothered with, because she didn't introduce herself. She didn't recognize me.

"Yeah, I'm their aunt," I replied. Her tone changed.

"Oh, okay! That's right, Palmer's sister right? I'm terrible with names..."

"Addie," I offered in return, "You're Katherine Holt's daughter, right? I think our mothers are friends."

"Of course! Addie! I'm Maureen." Having further assessed me and my appearance, she asked, "Home for the summer?"

"I actually just graduated."

"Oh, great!" she said.

By this point, we'd been flanked by the children who we came to pick up, and she'd lost interest in our conversation. We said our farewells, and I suffered through the last hour or so with the children before Nan returned, complaining that the butcher had been out of the specific cured meat that Palmer liked to eat as antipasti. When I got home and prepared to pass out on the sofa while watching some basic cable dreck, my mother came in and stared at me.

"Honey," she said, a tone of matronly concern in her voice, "Do we need to take you shopping?"

Whenever my mother thought I'd slept too long, she would come into my bedroom and open the blinds. I really hated her at those moments. On the days where opening the blinds was all she did, I got over it pretty quickly. Then there were the days where blind-opening turned into non-stop traffic in and out of my room, during which she would try to carry on a conversation with me as though I weren't sleeping. On the third such occasion the morning after my first day of playing nanny, she came in carrying a basket full of fresh-cut flowers from her garden.

"What are those for?"

"Oh, I thought they'd brighten up the pool house a bit. He's very brooding, you know. Needs a bit of color."

"I ran into Maureen Grant at camp."

"Oh, yes, her kids are about the same ages as Alex and Maddy. Oh, now, what are their names? The boy is called Tag short for Taggart; I gather that's a family name. Ainsley is the girl."

"Do you talk to Katherine much these days?"

"Oh, sure. You know, we go and have coffee or lunch or something and catch up almost every week."

I could picture it in my head, the two of them discussing who'd recently gotten a DUI over club sandwiches and iced tea.

Unsolicited, my mother now proceeded to update me on the lives of Katherine's three daughters, all in my age cohort. We've never been fast friends, but Mom seemed perpetually hopeful that at some point in our lives we'll find some common ground and become as sickeningly close as she and Katherine are.

"Well, so you saw Maureen. She's married to a dentist. I think he's got a private practice somewhere downtown, and they have the two little ones. They live right across from the elementary school. Then there's Meredith, she's about your age, right? She's finishing up another semester at Craft; I think she's in fashion merchandising or something, and she just got engaged to her boyfriend. It's really a cute story, they met at some mixer and he's going to go to med school or law school or something. Beautiful ring, huge diamond. Then, Megan is a junior or going to be a senior at the high school. Katherine's a little worried about her; she's too thin. She took her to the bakery last week and made her eat a whole piece of cake right in front of her."

"Mm. That sounds like it will definitely cure her eating disorder," I said.

"Well, you know, Addie, parenting isn't easy. She just did what she thought was best."

"So did Hitler."

"What?"

"Hitler did what he thought was best."

"Someday, when you're a mother, you'll understand," she replied, "Listen, I'm going to put the flowers in a vase and leave them in the kitchen. I'll text Eduardo and tell him to come get them. I'm going out."

An hour or so later, when I'd decided that I wasn't going to fall back asleep, I went to go get some breakfast. I hadn't thought about the fact that, once again, I was not wearing a bra, or pants that extended past my ass, until I came into the kitchen only to run square into the musician.

"Who are you?" he asked. Annoyed that this asshole had the nerve to question my presence in my own house, I responded, eyes narrowed.

"Ah, the daughter," he went on, "What's your story, huh?"

"What's my story?"

"What do you do with your life?"

"I'm taking care of my brother's kids," I replied, "How's the pool house?"

"Your mother's been kind to host me. I can see from your face that you'd rather I wasn't here."

I tried to be polite and explain that it wasn't him, that I was a chronic scowler, but he was right.

"How are you finding Ravine?" I asked, trying again.

"It's a beautiful place," he said, "full of beautiful people who are not happy."

"I'm sure the cultural norms are different here from Argentina."

"Yes. Also, I am not stupid."

Again, I found myself having to reassure him that that wasn't what I had meant. It was sort of what I meant, but to come right out and say that would have been offensive. I began aggressively pouring a bowl of cereal.

"You're angry," he said. I was.

"I'm not angry," I said, " I'm just trying to eat some fucking cereal."

"Mm," he said, "Well, thank your mother for the flowers for me," grabbing the vase and exiting the room.

"You can text her," I called as he waltzed out the back door and back into his cave. I was now caught between a rock and a hard place. On one hand, I could stay at my house and comfortably lounge but potentially have to deal with my mother and/ or Eduardo running play-by-plays of my emotional state. On the other hand, I could go to Gran's, where I wasn't likely to be bothered, but would have to at least feign working on job applications. I chose the latter.

My whole life I've tried to convince other people that just because I'm from Ohio doesn't mean I grew up in the middle of a cornfield without proper medical care or social niceties. Plodis is one of the bigger cities in the state, which I've always emphatically stated to anyone who would listen, and Ravine is simply an extension of Plodis. Ravine (only two square miles) itself may not be any bigger than one of those tiny farming hamlets vivisected by a desolate state route, but it is dressed in nicer clothes and within a larger metropolitan area. They took us on a field trip around the city in third grade: we learned the specific geographic bounds of our school system, and memorized the names of heroic settlers who had probably killed boatloads of people to lay claim to the land.

When it was first built, Gran and Pop's house was the only one for miles, and there was only one road into Ravine, so Pop's father could travel from his factory across the river to the house. That road leads to the town square now. In the Southeast corner of the city, the house and its grounds run into the river, which flows into Oak Lake at the edge of Gran and Pop's property. The north side of the city is where all the schools are. There is one elementary school, one junior high school, and one high school. All three buildings are great, brick, fortress-like buildings that take up one city block each and are divided only by side streets. West of the schools lie the athletic fields and natatorium, bordered by the community center, then City Park.

Ravine has the dual capacity to be both disheartening and familiar. Much like my family, Ravine was unique for inspiring both calm and discomfort in my person. That particular day, even though I had made an effort, and put on jeans rather than stretch leggings, stepping outside subjected me to potentially taxing social interaction. Not wanting to meet a community member who would smile and judge me all at once, I drove a perfectly walkable distance, up the tree-lined drive laid with fresh wood chips, to the house's isolated comfort. Gran opened the door and gave me a hug before asking if I was still doing dirty laundry accumulated at college. She was on her way out, but she told me about the hide-a-key in the cast-iron mailbox, so I could let myself out. The house was much more impressive when it was quiet and empty, the marble foyer cold and glistening, and the polished wood banister projecting a fortified importance.

Out of habit, I headed straight for the kitchen and opened the fridge. Gran always stocked it with beverages: two cans each of cream soda, root beer, and cola, a bottle of pinot grigio, a half-gallon glass bottle of whole milk, a glass pitcher of orange juice, and a carafe of iced tea. I thought for a second about drinking a root beer, but house rules dictated that I would have to go get another can from the basement to replace the one I'd taken and thus restore the symmetry. It didn't seem quite worth the effort. I surveyed the exterior of the fridge, which was plastered with a wedding invitation, a postcard from a neighbor who was spending the summer in Tuscany, and a printed invitation for the Mehn-ki-hil Tribe Heritage Celebration, a benefit for the original residents of the area, borne of delayed white guilt from seizing all the land and using it for industry. Pop's *Plodis Business Times* was open on the counter to the "30 under 30," article, featuring a girl who'd graduated a couple years ahead of me in high school and now ran a rapidly franchising and financially successful business. I sighed and walked down the hall to the house's library.

In order to thoroughly chronicle my job search, a binder had to be made. It's a habit I had picked up in college, excessive decoration of binders. Categorization made things less dire. It improved things which alcohol could not. Armed with paint pens and file tabs, I went to work, even turning on the massive CD player hidden in a cabinet to the classical music it always played. After about five minutes, I was done, quite impressed with my work. A once-dull office supply was painted with a pretty script spelling out "vocation," with viny flowers winding around it. My future prospects in life divided into tabs: Résumé, Cover Letters, Follow-Ups, and Interviews. I had a bunch of job listings bookmarked on my laptop, so now I had come to the inevitable, and highly unenjoyable, act of actually writing inquiries.

It was a favorite saying of my mother's mother, known colloquially as Kentucky Sue, that "Democrats do the devil's work." I feel that way about cover letters. Writing these generalized shouts into the void, so often borne of desperation, seems like the equivalent of showing up at a bar wasted and lonely, and telling anyone who'll grant you an aside that you give amazing blowjobs to get some attention. Maybe when Mom and Dad were young, this letter writing netted them a really good lay, a lifetime career. In the economy of my graduation, it was far more likely that a job netted by your cover letter, even after she'd behaved like a wanton harlot to garner attention, would be in a skeezy apartment with a guy who wouldn't even buy her coffee in the morning. Worse, every job available seemed the equivalent of some dirty old man trying desperately to make himself look like a ripped twenty-two-year-old who also happened to be smart, sensitive, and emotionally supportive. A job with GREAT benefits (shit pay), HUGE potential for promotion (you're at the bottom of the heap), and ENDLESS opportunities for learning to take place (training? what's that?). Turns out that just like a guy snuggled up to after multiple shots of tequila, that job was always single for a reason, and once you saw the backside of either in full daylight, you began hatching a plan to leave.

There was an old loveseat in the library, delicate looking and upholstered with dusty rose-colored velvet. I settled into it, entering a few sentences into the laptop while laying on my back. "A lifelong lover of the arts, I was pleased to hear of this position." *Please hire me.* "I believe my unique mix of experience, both educational and vocational, make me an ideal candidate for this position." *I can read.* "I am highly skilled at communications, both verbal and written." *I'm so great at answering phones.*

A spring in the sofa dug into my back, and somehow that minor discomfort gave me permission to check Facebook. I had a friend request from Tyler Hogue. A friend request might have had any number of meanings. Maybe it meant Tyler was legitimately interested in me, and maybe it meant he had a compulsive habit of friending everyone he had ever met. I told myself it didn't fucking matter. The boy with a pretty face and Kennedy hair who was making probably-empty overtures would blend together with the chump who bothered me while I ate cereal and the family that thought I dressed like a hobo as soon as I was employed and miles away.

As much as I had moved past the assorted (and relatively minor) social traumas of my childhood, its memories stuck with me, thoroughly insisting upon their continued relevance. There was a kid who fell asleep every single day in my fifth grade class. My gran insisted it was because he came from a large Catholic family and she was sure the requisite glut of siblings interfered with his sleep. The teacher used to wake him up and say, "The less sleep you get at night, the more time you have to prepare for the day." I remember feeling bad for him then, but those words were with me my second day of nannying at 5:30 in the morning. Anxious about life in general, I prepared for my day of suburban activity by compulsively making myself pretty and drinking cold coffee from the day before. First came my face, waxed, washed, toned, and moisturized. Sitting hunchbacked in front of a mirror, I patted on primer, foundation, and pressed powder. Blush could only go on if I was smiling, and then in two swooping strokes. A contoured eye: dark shadow in the crease and corner, a middling shade across the lid, a lighter shade applied in a thick stripe with an eyeliner brush, lighter still in the inner corner of the eyes and beneath the browbones. Then the eyeliner pencil, slightly above, then slightly below both lashlines. Mascara, applied at five different angles, eyes open, then closed, to get those wayward lashes in the corner. Extra concealer where I had picked too hard at blemishes in the past week. Lip balm to soften my lips, stain to color, and more balm. I put on the outfit I had picked out with care a couple of hours ago: cropped black cigarette pants, ballet flats, a printed silk blouse. I even took the time to choose accessories: pearl drop earrings and a delicate pendant. I straightened my posture, eyes straight ahead and looking through the mirror. I teased my hair into a nice fluffy bun, spritzed myself with perfume, made sure my hands were moisturized in case I had to shake anyone else's, and listened to some weepy pop music about how the singer was burdened by beauty. I thought I could be burdened with beauty if only I could contract some exotic disease and lose eighty pounds. Even with my girth, I had taken care of the flaws I could control, and felt a limited empowerment. I would be noticed, maybe even envied. Perfectly painted, I felt unstoppable. Either that, or my eyes were just too irritated by the makeup to see anything clearly.

"Ohhh, you look nice!" my mother crowed when I briefly walked through the kitchen on my way to Palmer and Nancy's, "Doesn't she look nice, Bob?"

"Uh-huh," he grunted, raising his eyebrows, but not actually lifting his eyeballs away from the gripping newspaper article he was reading. I both reveled in the compliment and hated that they secretly thought I would die a spinster if I wore leggings outside of the house. I hated that when I was in Ravine, I almost agreed with them.

The mood when I got to Palmer and Nan's was somehow subdued, but no less chaotic than the first day. Nan had bags under her eyes and moved a little more slowly to pack her gym bag, retrieving a tennis shoe from under the couch here, and her iPod from a charging deck there.

"The baby was up at like four this morning crying," she said, "He woke all the other kids up, and Palmer's been in Chicago for like thirty-six hours finalizing an important contract, so it's just been me. Literally all of them have been in my bed since Leo woke up, watching cartoons all morning. So they'll be tired, and I honestly wouldn't even try to take them to camp. They might freak out. I'm just off to the gym, then the spa, maybe a little grocery shopping."

"Okay," I said.

Okay is all that can ever be said to a hurried list of instructions that someone has blurted to you early in the morning. I soon realized that, without the carefully choreographed routine, I would actually have to interact with the older children.

"So, Leo woke up early today, huh?" I asked.

"Yes, he was crying and crying," said Madeleine.

"Maybe he had a bad dream," Alex interjected.

"Maybe," I said. Some sort of venture out of the house would be required if I were to keep my sanity. I found myself trying to think of locations that would both entertain the children and sell some form of caffeine. The Ravine Library had a coffee shop right next to it. The younger two strapped into a stroller, we set off for the library, which had at least different toys and different computers and different stories than home. I looked down, noting Leo's steely-eyed reserve not to fall asleep, though his eyelids drooped periodically. We ran into Maureen Grant outside.

"Cute flats, Addie!" she said

"Thanks," I replied, "They're from Target, but the little accents reminded me of Gucci."

She smiled sadly at me and gave a little wave before heading back to her car. Leo began to cry and wail "home," and as she drove away, I was sure I saw a smug smile on Maureen's face. I could dress the part, her face seemed to say, but everyone knew I was pretending. When I was young my mother would have let me cry, but then perhaps that was why I'd never been able to adjust to social norms.

"Listen, Leo," I said, trying to summon the words I supposed Gran might say, "Sometimes we've just got to do things we don't feel like doing. You'll have fun."

Fueled by espresso, my day, smudged with eyeliner and cigarette pants and flats that reminded me of couture even as their cheap rubber soles betrayed them, would be fine.

"Addie…hey…" said Tyler Hogue. Did he live there or something?

"Hey," I replied, doing my best not to sound like I hated the world.

"Whose kids are these?" he asked.

"Oh, my brother's. Palmer's and Nan's. I've been helping out with them until one of those real job things comes along. How are you?"

"Good. Good. I was offered a summer associate position at Daedalus Financial."

"Oh! That's where my family works."

"I know. Hey, listen, you like artsy things right?"

"Sure," I said, slightly bemused.

"They're showing a silent movie at the Plodis Theatre on Saturday, and of course none of my friends want to come. Would you be interested in seeing that? I think its Lillian Gish, or Louise Brooks, or something."

Had I heard correctly? Had the admittedly beautiful and Ivy-educated classmate who I still viewed as a shallow, preppy fuck just asked me out? There had to be a catch, but if I had stayed silent any longer to figure it out I would have looked like an idiot.

"Yeah, okay, " I said in spite of myself.

"What's your number?" he said, whipping out his phone. It

wasn't the attention I'd had in mind when I had contoured my cheekbones that morning, but it would do.

It seems so innocuous, the act of asking someone out. In most of the world, it might have been. But there were those child-hood traumas again. There were several occasions I could remem-ber from my adolescence where asking someone out had been re-duced to little more than competition for a trophy. Surveys on the playground, lists compiled on the bus to Washington D.C. Tyler had never been an instigator in these situations, but my childhood mood map connected him inexorably to this culture. From each encounter that fundamentally objectified me or anyone around me resulted a distinct patch of emptiness. Over time I had stitched them together into some sort of quilt, a barrier that made me pause when exposed to any kind of vulnerability. I wanted desperately to shed this second skin, but underneath I was naked, and the same things that had built up my walls told me I wasn't worthy of love without them. Enjoying life without worry that it would leave me empty was an eternal challenge.

Later that day, I made lunch for the kids. Sandwiches cut into dinosaur shapes with pretty cookie cutters, and halved grapes, and crimped carrot medallions, and milk that hadn't been treated with anything untoward and came in a glass jug. I put things that had been haphazardly left on the kitchen counter into size-appropriate piles, and threw random bits of dirty laundry down the chute. I sprayed down surfaces with some sort of non-toxic cleaner and compacted the trash and let the dog out for a nice romp in the yard. For a fleeting moment, I thought that maybe this sense of order was Ravine's version of happiness. Nan came through the back door, puffy-eyed, and I was allowed to go.

"Addie," she called after me, "You look cute today!"

I appreciate feminism. In Ohio—hell, in the world—saying that you appreciate feminism to the wrong person labels you as a man-hater who burns bras and thinks *Interior Scroll* is the greatest artwork of all time. In reality, what I mean is that while I like to cook, I hate the idea of having to serve dinner at a specific time for a generic husband. While I would like to be treated like a human, not just a woman, I also require a pretty heavy-duty underwire. Pre-feminism, I assume, someone actually asked you out for a "date," a steak dinner, and you knew that the end-game was marriage. Post-feminism—evidently—someone asked you if you liked to do artsy things. You agreed to an outing not really knowing whether they sincerely just didn't want to attend a cultural event alone, or whether they'd try to get in your pants, or whether they'd never paid attention to women's issues, and were auditioning you for the role of girlfriend, or fiancé, or wife.

It had been my experience in Ravine that my impassioned defenses of human rights and feminism mostly made people uncomfortable. I was no stranger to the shifty eye contact and shrugging shoulders people might otherwise reserve for doomsday proclaimers on the street. I had just recently gotten to the point where I could get through a regular conversation without one of these responses occurring. Dates required a lot more effort. They required an understanding of social cues, remembering manners, and appearing witty. They're something normal people do, and I'm not normal. Difference has clung to me my entire life, like some horribly static poly-blend.

Once I figured out that I couldn't just wear a flowery dress, speak my mind, and have someone perfect fall in love with me (circa tenth grade) I began to withdraw. I didn't do love. I didn't do vulnerability. I didn't even like for people to see me cry. I learned to hide my emotions. In the celebrated cemetery of Ravine, I knew I was living among sadness and death, but to openly acknowledge this fact would have been blasphemy of some sort. So I learned not to emote when another funeral procession passed by (the boy I had a crush on started doing drugs), I learned to sing cheerfully to a dirge (yes, that story about a girl drunkenly falling down stairs is hi-larious), I learned to react to epilogues as though they were forewords (reform school's really the best thing for Bobby), and I learned to walk around the headstones, so that, even as they filled my life, I could act as though they weren't there. Ravine taught me that if I didn't care about things, I wouldn't hurt when they died. Lennie said via text that my outing with Tyler was a date. I said I didn't care. I tried not to care. But I had already sent her pictures of possible outfits, and we'd decided on a plain, cornflower blue dress. My eyes were appropriately smoky, my legs shaved. I cared.

He pulled up in his Beemer a few minutes late, windows rolled down in the relative coolness of the summer dusk. Effortlessly classic in a striped oxford with the sleeves rolled up, fitted khakis, and some sort of driving loafers, he smiled at me as I climbed in the passenger side. It seemed weird for me to be in the same car as someone who I had previously associated only with passing conversation at scholarship banquets, and secret, misplaced hatred.

"How was your run?" I asked, referencing earlier correspondence.

"Good," he replied almost reflexively, gnawing on a grey-looking protein bar, "It was good. Did you babysit today?"

"No. I only do that like three days a week. I worked on job applications for a while and caught up with a friend from school."

In reality, I had looked at job listings for twenty minutes then lazily texted Lennie while I watched TV.

"Cool. That sounds nice."

"What did you do today?"

"Today was actually pretty good. I got to go to a business plan competition with my supervisor to discuss socially responsible investment, so that was a nice break from the office. What kind of jobs are you looking at?"

"Oh, you know, mostly research-y things at universities that I have no chance in hell of getting because I only have undergrad."

"Political science-related?"

"Yeah, splinter groups and ideological factions and the like."

"So you'd be a protector of the realm type, right? Making sure no one gets too out of control?"

"I guess," I replied, laughing because that seemed the only appropriate response to such verbiage.

We were crossing the river now, the "natural" boundary between Ravine and Plodis, and the only route possible to reach the Plodis Theatre. Built back in the twenties before people ran out of money, it was one of those grand and opulent old theaters that had once been wallpapered with velvet, and was still graced with random bits of gold filigree and stained glass and exotic animals people had killed on safari and stuffed. It survived on the dole of an unknown wealthy benefactor and proceeds from screenings of old movies meant to draw in hipsters and the elderly. Fun fact about silent movies: they're the same length as regular movies. I don't know why I thought it would be short, but it was an hour and a half long. In a way, I suppose you never remember movies you see on dates. Even though I was moderately interested in what was happening on screen for the first fifteen minutes, I was equally concerned with appearing to be enjoying it in case of any sideways glances from Tyler, to laugh charmingly at the funny parts, and to smile beatifically at any of the cute little filmic details present only in such early films. I wanted to look engaged and pretty enough so that he could gaze admiringly at me throughout the film and become more enchanted with me as it progressed.

As much as the me of high school gloom could not entertain the idea of this coupling becoming anything significant, the dreamer hidden away deep beneath my ribs was playing a second movie in my head. In my head, I was in a beautiful gown and Tyler was telling me that he knew I was the one that first night when we went to see Lillian Gish at the theatre and that each time I had laughed he'd fallen a little more in love with me. That when a single, solitary tear rolled down my cheek, he knew he'd never be happy with another. I had drowned myself in the realism of cheap cocktails for the last four years, but all the rubbing alcohol in the world wouldn't kill my flights of fancy, and so I tried simply not to grant them weight, even as they unfolded rapturously in my thoughts.

After the movie ended, we walked back to the underground parking garage and he suggested going for something to eat. We bonded over the gross couple that had been seated in front of us.

"Save some for later," I said, thinking myself somehow witty despite the fact that that is a stock line from every romantic comedy made in the mid-1990s.

We ended up at a little bistro known for its locally sourced vegetables and healthy fare, and I found myself specifying that we needed a table for two to the hostess, feeling so adult, so formal. The metallic mesh chairs were cold against the backs of my legs, and I was sure that there would be some sort of geometric pattern covering my thighs after. We ordered beer, even though I hate beer, and ate some rice-based salad laid on a bed of greens. It was mediocre, but I said it was delicious. We talked about our families. His mother was away at a silent yoga retreat, forever attempting to balance her chakras. His father escaped by playing golf and litigating all over the country. His parents were crazy. That's so funny, because mine were too. Laughter came more easily, eye contact lingered for a while longer each time our eyes met. As he pulled into my parents' driveway and put the car in park, we were condemned to the awkward silence appropriated to the last moments of any first date. I hate awkward silence, and so I leaned in for a quick peck, thanked him for a good time, and turned to get out.

"Wait," he said softly.

I turned, and there it was: one, two, three solid kisses. These weren't sloppy "too drunk to care" kisses, either. They were good kisses, kisses that left a little buzz on my lips. I had to remind myself to make eye contact and offer a soft promise of future contact as I got out of the car, rather than my requisite "See ya." I walked in the back door, not even caring that Eduardo was sitting on the patio, lurking and smoking a cigarillo. My mother, brewing her nighttime tea, told me I looked pretty in a clipped tone of voice, but for once, the sharp tone of her words seemed to fade a little bit into the background. I lay in my bed, looking straight up at the cracking cream paint on the ceiling, and basking in the thought that maybe, just maybe, I'd be a late bloomer instead of something weird and leafy that most people only use as filler between the roses.

First kisses are funny things, aren't they? They make you forget how disgusting exchanging saliva with another person is. They make you feel a little bit superior when you recount them, in particular detail, to your friend on the phone. In my case, they also meant avoiding my mother, who was bound to ask snidely why I had such a skip in my step, and my father, who would put on an affected look of disinterest whenever my mother quizzed me about boys.

"Well, you look like you're in a good mood today!" Nan chirped as I entered the house the next morning.

"So, what you're saying is that I don't normally look like I'm in a good mood."

"Oh, no. That's not what I meant. You do look awfully pained sometimes, though. Now, Alex and Maddy are at camp till two…" She launched into the daily directive. Those days where nothing special happened tend to blend together. I suppose I built block towers and watched terrible children's television and drank too much non-dairy creamer in my coffee. I only know that I began to feel as though I might finally have assumed a well-dressed and socially functional role in my community. Accordingly, most of the time, things didn't enrage or annoy me just as much as they didn't thrill me. On days off, I went to the house, lounged in the library, and didn't mind replacing the drinks in the fridge, nor the fact that I wasn't getting much done.

On one of these dreamy, foggy days, I found myself—in spite of my desire to take on the world—unable to focus on uploading my résumé to websites where I would also have to copy and paste it into stupid little dialogue boxes. I pulled an old book from the shelf behind me, a canvas-bound first edition that smelled like it had been perpetually damp for about sixty years. I opened to a random page, hoping for some wise pronouncement about life. BRIIIIIIIINGGGG. I dropped the book, startled. It was Lennie.

"He-ey," I answered.

"Hey, girl. How are you? What's happening?"

"Nothing much, just working on job apps. How's Purge?"

"Fucking awful, Addie. My boss is like a nightmare stage-mother, but she's frigid and single and childless, so we all get the brunt of it."

"Sounds fun."

"She called a girl from Accounting 'heinously ugly' the other day. Like, I'm sorry, are we not adults? The girl can't fucking help it. Ugh. And she dyes her hair this awful dark red color and only likes me because I'm pretty and obsessive-compulsive."

"Well, it's a hard job, Lennie, but someone's got to do it."

"Shut up. How's the boy? Are you gonna hang out again?"

"I don't even know. We text back and forth, but neither of us has proposed a second date. I'm at Palmer and Nancy's half the time, and I come to my grandparents' house to work on stuff and avoid my mother."

"Make the first move! How's taking care of the kids going?"

"Fine. They're fine. I'm not going to be able to do it forever, though. I need to get out of here. What's going on with you?"

"Remember my high-school boyfriend Brian? He totally broke my heart like five years ago?"

"Uh-huh."

"I ran into him and we started talking and, you know, next thing you know we're sitting on his kitchen floor smoking weed and talking about how amazing it is that we've found each other again."

I didn't follow. It wasn't that amazing. They'd grown up in the same town and then moved back.

"Wow," I said, "So are you guys seeing each other?"

"I'm practically spending every night at his apartment," she said. "The sex is so much better than in high school."

"Well, at least there's that."

"I know this sounds completely insane," she continued, "But I'm thinking he could be the one. I mean, he just got back from working with refugees in Africa. I'm smitten."

"Good," I said, knowing it would fall apart in a couple months.

"Yeah. I have to go sort through fabric swatches, but date soon, okay?"

"Okay, sounds good."

"K. Loveyoubye."

Just exactly after I hung up the phone, I heard Gran's voice. Fuck. They weren't supposed to be home yet. I hadn't replaced my pop in the fridge. Fuck. I rushed to put the book back on the shelf, when I noticed that a slip of painfully thin, antiqued looking paper was peeking out from between its pages. It was old; the handwriting was delicate and fine. It read:

"Picked berries today with delicious abandon. Carelessness is a luxury, and one that allows us to be surrounded by green, to contemplate which of the best and brightest shades of pink must cross our lips. Youth is the pinprick of light shining through tree branches, a small crack in the treacle that hardens as the day grows later."

I wanted more time with it, but I replaced it and put the book back on the shelf, paranoid that—just as she would notice a can out of place in her perfectly organized fridge—Gran would notice the slightest change to the makeup of her library. Root beer needed to be moved. Furthermore, I wanted a little time to contemplate the possibilities of the note to myself. I was nearly certain that if I brought it up to anyone in the family, it would be swiftly discredited or explained away. Anything resembling a flight of fancy was. Whoever had written it seemed as though they had enjoyed life, something that I needed to learn how to do properly. I put it back on the shelf, though its words were firmly planted in my heart.

In the 1700s, before Plodis was anything more than a dusty mill town, and before Ravine existed at all, there was a bloodbath here. Like everywhere else in this country, there were people here who didn't want to just give everything up, people who had ownership over the land: the Mehn-ki-hil tribe of Native Americans. Like everywhere else, they were defeated and survivors were forced to move to less profitable land up north. Ravinites weren't taught that in school. They taught us about the great, old industrial power of Adriel Weston, and every year, like a good little acolyte, I'd brought in some family relic, a letter written to my great-grandfather Adriel from the mayor of Plodis, a fascinating part of the past brought to light. There was a sense of pride attached to sharing names with someone historic and significant. Plenty of people stop there, never realizing that people whom history tends to remember quite often stood for terrible things. I, on the other hand, felt guilty for broad actions in which I'd had no part. Someone similarly afflicted with residual white guilt years back made a scholarship for the descendants of the Mehn-ki-hils. The Weston family became a prime contributor to the cause, and Gran likes to keep up appearances, which was the reason, more than anything, that I was in a modest little black dress and pearls a few nights later, awkwardly mingling with Ravine's most charitable citizens in Gran and Pop's ballroom. Katherine Holt approached.

"Hi honey," she said, wrapping me in a taffeta hug, "I know you've been taking care of the kids. Maureen said she's seen you dropping them off at camp."

"Yeah, it's been a nice thing to have while I'm looking for something that actually relates to my degree."

"Now, remind me of what you majored in, hon."

"Political Science and I minored in History."

"Oh, okay, so what kind of job are you looking for again?"

"Well, I wrote my thesis on unsuccessful revolutions, so I guess I'd like to explore that further."

"So grad school's on the horizon?"

"Oh, eventually. I want to be sure of what I want to study before I spend a lot of money on a Masters."

"Sure, sure. Well, listen, I won't keep you from mingling. I'm sure I'll see you around, huh?"

I smiled before she walked away. I hoped I wouldn't see her around. However, it was the nature of my mother's relationship with Katherine that they expounded upon, then justified each other's questionable parenting decisions. Regardless of my personal contact with her, she would undoubtedly hear about whatever direction my life took.

Suddenly, without warning, Gran was at my elbow, mur-

muring minor criticisms of the other guests into my ear. Gran's full name was Caroline Elaine Hoff Weston, though I'd only ever known people to call her Crisp. When people heard her called Crisp, they automatically assumed that she was from some East Coast, blueblood family, that there was some charming anecdote to explain the nickname, or a dear departed relative who bestowed such a moniker. Neither of those things existed. For every Punch or Glee that's come by their nickname honestly, there's another Chick or Elfie who's simply pretending that they have. Gran was a pretender. She had come from wealth to be sure, but it wasn't— as it turned out—legally obtained. She'd lived in Brooklyn as a child, before her father bought a house on Long Island. Though forbidden to speak of it, my mother once let slip that Gran's father was a bootlegger during Prohibition, that the money had kept them afloat during the Depression and had ultimately facilitated Gran's marriage to Pop, the heir to a flagging industrial fortune. As for her nickname, Gran had her father's degenerate past and slightly endearing simplicity to thank for that. He liked his money, and he loved his daughter. As he preferred the former new and crisp, he made sure to name the latter accordingly, hoping that the luck he had bought with crisp dollar bills might slink its way into her life. Rather than embracing her father's simplistic capitalist social strategy, Gran spent the latter part of her adolescence distancing herself from his humble beginnings, first at a boarding school in Virginia, then at Bryn Mawr. She loved and clung to convention like a scared girl, because it was her choice. Well into her eighties, she imposed her own rules at whim to ensure that her social standing remained at its peak.

Her strawberry blonde hair was always pulled into a thin chignon. Though she had quit smoking cigarettes years ago, the discarded habit was visible in the delicate creases that lined her face. She still took great pains with her appearance, applying thick coats of alabaster makeup and finishing powder, emphasizing her Bette Davis eyes with thick black eyeliner and multiple coats of expensive mascara, and dabbing her lips with light pink, non-ostentatious lipstick. Her engagement ring, a large, pointy diamond, shone menacingly from her manicured hands.

"What did she want?" Gran asked, watching Katherine move to her next unwitting victim.

"Oh, to know what I'm doing," I replied.

Gran huffed, "Did you tell her to worry about the fact that her own daughter doesn't eat? Now, come along, there are people I think you might like."

I had learned long ago not to try escaping Gran's social introductions. Mention of anxiety did not faze her; she didn't believe in it. "You're fine," she would say. I am sure that she'd told my father the same thing, probably even told herself from time to time. They were both believers in liquid courage, and as far as I could tell, it worked for them. I was being led toward a group of suits. As I was wont to do, I calmed my social anxiety by reciting to myself the topics that I could discuss with them: return on investment, American League baseball, the weather. Gran tapped one of them on the shoulder.

"Tyler, I believe you know my granddaughter, Adelaide." Oh shit. Tyler Hogue, whom I'd neither seen nor had another invitation from since our nice, buzzy kisses.

"Yes, Mrs. Weston. How's it going, Addie?"

Gran spoke before I could answer, "I do wish you would give up going by Addie. Abbreviating names is for small children and the middle class."

"Ok, Gran," I replied. It was useless to argue. Gran made up some reason to float away from us, and the worst ensued: I had to make small talk not knowing whether or not he wanted to run away.

"So," I said, "How's Daedalus?"

"Good," he replied, laughing at the impersonal turn my conversational skills had taken, "How are those kids?"

"Pretty cute," I replied painfully.

Gran was back, this time with another youngish-looking woman in tow.

"This is my granddaughter, Adelaide, and her friend, Tyler," Gran said, imposing social relations she hoped would come to pass, "This is Adrienne, this year's scholarship recipient. I thought I would rescue her from the old ladies and introduce her to you."

Adrienne, a vaguely Mediterranean-looking girl ("She doesn't look like an Indian," Gran had whispered), wearing a modest, flowered dress, smiled shyly as we exchanged pleasantries. She would be attending State University in the fall, studying business. She could trace her Mehn-ki-hil heritage back four generations and worked in an ice cream shop on the weekends. Eventually, she was dragged up to the front of the room, where remarks were made. People didn't stop talking, in their champagne-fluted clusters of twos and threes. The aim here was for attendees to enjoy themselves; the cause was secondary. To be wholly altruistic just wasn't in most Ravinites' composition. The idea of helping a disadvantaged girl attend college sounded very nice, but their carefully constructed and highly specialized lives didn't allow for any true interruptions. And so, they flocked to each benefit not because they were passionate about changing anything, necessarily, but because it was a party that fulfilled certain requirements. Galas had to be close to Ravine, they had to have an open bar, and there had to be something to occupy those in attendance (if possible, an additional opportunity to spend money, most likely a silent auction). The contributions were mostly a drop in the bucket for Ravine residents, and not in any way a lasting commitment to resolving any problem. The only troubles in the world that were made visible were those that would never affect its residents, and the market value of the clothes being worn and spirits being drunk was collectively more than the total raised for the charity by the end of the night.

Goodness was measured differently here. In spite of Gran's silver-tongued criticisms of guests, she was allowing them to use her home, so her good intent could not be denied outright. Others measured their virtue by all the nasty thoughts they kept themselves from saying aloud. If they neglected to point out an ugly dress, a flabby arm, a substance abuse episode, this made them more benevolent. In a year's time, no one would remember Adrienne's name, nor any of the conversations they had had here.

"Hey," Tyler leaned over and whispered in my ear, "When can I see you again?"

JULY

M ost Midwesterners are proud, if not of our current democracy, of the rose-colored intentions we suppose the
Founding Fathers must have had. We like Francis Scott Key and
his romantic wording even as we know that in modern warfare the
flag would have been incinerated before midnight. Because we'd
rather eat imitation whipped cream and berries, three-bean salad,
and charred hot dogs than debate policy or try to do anything about
it, we take to the streets each Fourth of July, celebrating the freedoms we pretend haven't been tragically maimed. In true American fashion, Ravinites head to the town square an hour before the
Independence Day parade to stake out viewing posts with cheap
lawn chairs around the town square.

When I was younger, I'd follow my father up the block,
perching on the curb with neighbor kids as he cleaned his clip-
on sunglasses with a handkerchief and readied his camera to take
photos of the marching bands and flatbed floats. He still did that
the year after college, but instead of going with him and sitting for

an hour looking across the street at other people in lawn chairs, I opted for an extra thirty minutes of sleep. By the time I got downstairs, Mother had already disappeared with her stainless steel water bottle and high SPF foundation slathered on her face, which left only Eduardo sitting dejectedly on the front porch staring at the passersby.

The sidewalk in front of our house was an amalgam of different squares. An ode to the progression of cement engineering, each one's appearance was dependent on when the roots of trees that the city had overzealously planted disrupted the last concrete pour. When we were younger and mom made a big deal of the holidays, she would string up a skeleton from the giant magnolia tree in front of the house each Halloween. She must have told Eduardo about this because there were microphones hanging from the exact same branch that July. He sat, on our shiny wicker furniture, surveilling Ravinites as they went cheerfully to the square, lawn chairs in tow. He looked out of place, wearing fitted chinos, a dark, long-sleeved button-down and driving mocs, clutching a mug of black coffee and letting a cigarillo slowly burn out between the index and middle finger of his other hand. Pedestrians would cough or crinkle their noses from time to time when they caught a whiff.

"Shouldn't you be asking people's permission to record them?" I asked.

"No."

"What if someone sues you?"

"Nobody's going to sue me. They wouldn't recognize their

own voices anyway."

"That's quite a superior attitude for you to take."

"You call me superior? You're the one drinking iced coffee."

"It is eighty degrees out," I rebutted, before sighing, shaking my head, and deciding that conversation was futile. Still, if I left now I'd be sitting in the direct sunlight for at least thirty minutes, talking to the likes of Katherine Holt. I stayed.

"Your coffee," Eduardo said after a fashion, "is actually quite fitting on this occasion. Soon, it will be diluted, just like this empty patriotism."

I knew he was only trying to get a rise out of me. A more refined person might have ignored him.

"I studied political science," I said, somehow thinking this would shut him up.

"Yes, your mother said," he responded. Well, goddammit. The prick was still speaking, "She said something about revolutions. If you ask me, you should try to start one instead of reading books about it."

"Jesus, you are insufferable," I said. He almost smiled. I was pretty well convinced that his image as a tortured artist wouldn't allow for an unabashed grin. I remained silent. I knew he was right, of course. Even as I fought with him, I knew that most of the people who sat watching the parade had never had to militantly defend their beliefs. I knew that the principle of equality was in direct opposition to everyone half-assedly clapping as marching bands from Plodis languished in the disgusting heat. But what

Eduardo didn't understand, and what I was all too aware of, was that this was America. If we acknowledged all the bad shit that went on inside our borders, we did it on our own terms, and not because some foreigner didn't understand our carefully woven web of denial. Besides, if Ravine had instilled anything in me, for better or worse, it was a deep-seated conviction not to take shit from anyone.

"I suppose my mother mentioned that my coursework was all related to failed revolutions?" I asked.

"She did."

"Well, then you'll have to forgive my cynicism, and the simplicity of my corn-eating brethren. People around here like to be associated with the winning team, you see. Those of us who know the foibles of victory also know that the active brand of patriotism you are so fervently advocating usually crashes and burns."

"Well," he responded, "Have you ever tried to start a revolution?"

"Please. I've considered starting a revolution since I was twelve. I wrote articles about fighting the patriarchy in my fourth-grade class newsletter. It's not as simple as just wanting to do it. Besides, I don't see you protesting anything."

"My apathy is my protest."

I laughed out loud.

"In your studies," he continued, "Did you ever come across a man named Leandro Alem?"

"Yes," I said, surprised that he actually knew something solid, "Revolución del Parque, July, 1890."

"You'll have read his suicide note?" he snidely added.

"No," I said, unapologetically.

"He was convinced that his passivity had led to the failure of the revolución, and so, rather than be alive and passive, he ended his life."

"That's fascinating," I replied, wondering where this conversation was going, "Now, we'd better head to the square or we'll miss the parade."

"Oh, I'm not going," Eduardo said.

"Why? Because there will be actual music there?" I asked, half-laughing to make my words seem less harsh.

"No," he said, "Because it is an empty display of patriotism."

"You know," I concluded, "No matter how valid your ideas, if your delivery sucks, no one cares."

"I don't care if people care."

I shook my head and huffed as I walked down the front steps. I stood by my first impression: he was a jerk.

By the time I reached the square, and the particular patch of grass and curb that my father had customarily lain claim to, Palmer, Nan, and the kids were already there. Dad was standing with a neighbor, discussing an Initial Public Offering. He hadn't chosen finance as a career, per se. It was the thing that made the most sense for him to pursue. It was what Pop did; a sort of family business.

"Hi Addie," he said hurriedly before turning back to the neighbor, "That IPO is bananas. The execs at that place must be going crazy. It's like: Happy Fourth of July, guys!"

A bass drum was audible in the distance and people began to abandon conversations and return to their assigned lengths of roadside.

Sitting on the curb with the children was decidedly less comfortable than lounging in a canvas chair, but on the curb I could pretend that I was coaching the children on how to get the cheap candy people threw from floats and dodge the inevitable questions about whether I had a boyfriend and when I planned to find a job. I had Leo on my lap like a shield. Lining either side of the street were clumps of Ravinites: those who wore matching American Flag t-shirts and sat in matching plastic chairs, those who looked like they'd rather be dead but came anyway and smiled grimly at their compatriots. Loads of people for me to avoid. So I laughed along at the children as they goofed off, stealing glances at Nan and Palmer interacting with people like normal adults and sipping out of cans ensconced in awful neoprene coozies. The parade passed as it always had, and as I am sure it still does.

It was the nature of being Gran's grandchild that every major holiday was pretty much scheduled for me. It was understood that, post-parade, after everyone had sufficiently chilled themselves in the air conditioning for a couple of hours, we would troupe over to Gran and Pop's backyard for a "garden party." I don't know why it was called that, but it always had been. Tricolor bunting was strewn across the terrace and small American flags had been stuck into the lawn between croquet, bocce, and badminton sets. There was a white, rented tent that had hired help beneath it, cooking burgers and hot dogs on a grill, and serving people cold drinks from an open bar. Gran had hired some high-schooler to sit on the part of their property that bordered Oak Lake so kids could go swimming there and no one would drown. On such occasions, I was obligated to traverse the expanse of gaudy, green grass, cheerfully engaging in conversation with anyone and everyone. My favorites were the senile old folks like Fred Lacey. As of late, I learned, he'd been reading a lot of dystopian literature and was warming to the idea of a society that assigned roles and skimped on personal freedoms, which drove his wife nuts.

"How are your kids?" I asked, attempting to redirect the conversation. His wife, Betty, looked like she was about to answer me, but her husband pre-empted her.

"They're horrible bastards," he said, "Shining examples of the society in which we raised them. You know, when I was growing up, it was understood that I would go into business. My father worked at Second National Trust, you know, before that business in seventy-eight when they dove right into the trashcan."

"Fred, she wasn't even born in seventy-eight," his wife barked.

"Aah, well, then you'll like this story. When I say the company dove into the trash, I'm being both literal and figurative. They found that my father's successor was embezzling, and he tried to commit suicide by jumping out his office window. It was an alley-facing office, though, and the poor shmuck landed right on top of a full dumpster. Didn't even break a rib. Anyway, what was I talking about, Betty?"

"Our children and how you hate them," she replied sardonically. He made a dismissive gesture toward her and continued his diatribe.

"Anyway, when I was a boy, my father was always telling me that I was going to go to the finest school in the country. He had done it, and it was my turn to write an essay on financial reformers and go to some skyscraper on Wall Street or Madison Ave and work like a dog until I died. So I did. I went to Princeton and I worked at a bank, and I hated my job. When Betty and I had kids, I said, We'll let them do anything they want. For Christ's sake, major in art, I don't care. All the good schools have meaningless degrees, I said, follow your dreams. They never appreciated the gift that I was giving them."

"Fred, calm down," Betty interjected, "Go get yourself a beer." He did not.

"I wanted my children to have choices and they completely, pardon my French, fucked it up. I mean, Betty, I didn't encourage Johnny to take art classes so he could scam people out of money and get shut down by the SEC. If he had studied art, you think he'd be involved in a Ponzi scheme? Adelaide, you ever read Ayn Rand?"

Having narrowly escaped an extended lecture from Mr. Lacey, I wandered to the food tent and loaded a sturdy but disposable bamboo plate with the usual variety of mayonnaise and carbohydrate-based salads, cold fruits and veggies, and charred meat before I was intercepted by Gran.

"I saw you talking to the Laceys," she said under her breath, "He's driving Betty nuts with all this Communist malarkey. He should talk to your mother's artist."

I smiled, not quite knowing how to respond. She continued scanning the crowd with her eyes, sipping wine out of a mini-bottle through a straw.

"Katherine Holt is pretending she's allergic to gluten. She asked me if I had any gluten-free ice cream sandwiches. Didn't her mother teach her to eat what she was given?"

"I think she actually went to the hospital for that."

"Nonsense. Nobody had these 'intolerances' when I was growing up. It's all in her head. Excuse me, darling, Linda's just gotten here and I haven't seen her since the surgery."

My father and Kaye were standing at the edge of the forest by themselves and I went to join them.

"Gran's convinced that Katherine Holt is faking her gluten intolerance," I said.

"Probably is," Dad said from the side of his mouth before taking a generous swig of beer.

"Where's the fam?" I asked Kaye.

"Oh, George probably went home already. I sent Darwin to swim in the lake, but he probably snuck home, too. He's so much like George." She gulped down a gin and tonic, "I ought to make

Dar live here over the summer. Mother could shame him into being more social, I'm sure."

"Leave the kid alone," Dad scoffed, "Addie, have you seen your mother?"

"No," I said, "but I'm about to leave. I could tell her you're looking for her if she's at home."

"Don't worry about it. I'll text her," he said, rolling his eyes and drinking the rest of his beer, "Another drink, sis?"

My food nearly finished, I left for home, and comfortable temperatures.

Tyler had invited me to watch the Ravine fireworks with him that night. I told myself that I had accepted his invitation so I wouldn't have to watch them with my parents. In truth, I was already a little in love with him. In Ravine, it had always been easier to live in my head. And so, like some people saved seeds, in tiny glass jars that were labeled and alphabetized, I saved tiny parallel worlds. They were incomplete and imperfect but they waited, somewhere in my brain, for me to pluck one of them out of the abyss and unite it with actuality. I conjured stories based upon a sentence here or there between an acquaintance and myself, or that one time when a stranger at the coffee shop looked sad, and I thought, wouldn't it be curious if beneath his enviable complexion was a layer of person that only I could see? That was my problem, of course, having a million dream worlds inside my head. It meant that every person I had ever met, I fell a little in love with. Even if I hated them, there was always a possibility that they were only awful because they had never really been loved by anybody and wouldn't it be beautiful and wonderful if I, Adelaide Weston, was the one thing that could make them smile instead of frown? And so, for my entire life, while boys had been thinking that I was pretty or that I had big boobs, I had been painting mental images of myself cooking roast for them and our four children. They still brought me daisies home from work, even though we were forty.

I alternately longed for and feared the constructed surrealism I used to process life. That was the really big thing Lennie and I had in common: constantly wanting the world and being a little afraid of it at the same time. The only way either of us knew how to cope was self-sabotage. My default was inaction, hers was impulsive action. Yet here I was, about to have a second date with Tyler.

Tyler's parents lived next door to Gran and Pop, so walking up their nearly identical driveway at dusk was strangely familiar. They had a nice, stone house, which I bypassed to get to Tyler's "apartment," the second floor of their carriage-house turned garage. I had misgivings about the whole business. For every falls-in-love dream world I collected, there was always the nearly identical falls-in-love-only-to-discover-he's-a-serial-killer world. The fact that I was in Ravine tipped the scales largely in the latter direction. I saw the headline flash before my eyes, "Fat Blonde Found in Shallow Grave After Agreeing to Date with Yale Grad."

This paranoia was not helped when Tyler appeared at the door with a tote slung over his arm and led me into the forest. Oh, well. If it was my time to go, at least I'd be murdered by someone who was overqualified and well-dressed. We were almost to the river before he motioned overhead to a treehouse. This wasn't like a Little Rascals treehouse that Spanky and Alfalfa cobbled together out of plywood, either. It was Swiss Family Robinson up in that motherfucker. His father must have been very successful as a lawyer, because they had clearly hired a skilled carpenter to make a legitimate house that was bigger than my bedroom in a tree. As we climbed the spiral staircase that had been built around the tree trunk, I began to blurt questions:

"How did I not know about this? Did your parents build this?"

"Yeah, they built it for me and my sisters during their separation. They'd send us out here when they wanted to fight in the house."

Yikes.

"How many sisters do you have?" I asked.

"Just the two. Susanna's twenty-five and Gretchen's sixteen."

"This is extraordinary," I exclaimed still taken aback at where I was. It was a plain room, yes, but it had electrical hookups and an entire set of furniture.

"They really liked to fight," he replied.

"When was their separation?" I asked.

"When we were in high school."

"That sucks, but they're still together, right?"

"Tax reasons," he said, pulling a box of Cracker Jack and a couple bottles of Pellegrino out of his tote.

"You do not have Cracker Jack," I gasped.

"Oh, I have Cracker Jack," he said with a smile, "The question is whether I intend to let you have any."

I feigned insult. How could he have known I would have fought to the death for a sugar-encrusted snack? I sat on the couch next to him and laughed.

"What?" he said.

"I don't know," I said, "This. The fact that I am sitting in the treehouse of a king and eating Cracker Jack with you."

"What? You never imagined this in tenth grade English class when you were doodling on your college-ruled paper?"

I tried to smile. There were a lot of things I could smile convincingly at that I didn't think were funny, but high school wasn't one of them.

"You really didn't like high school, huh?"

"Oh, I don't know," I said, trying to play off my unattractive malaise, "I guess I felt like it was just something I had to get through, not enjoy."

"I didn't like it either, you know," he said. I must have rolled my eyes, "You don't believe me?"

"I guess you just always seemed like you were having fun."

"I mean, the whole time Mom and Dad were a mess, and school was stable, I guess. But I wouldn't say I enjoyed it. I think everybody was just trying to get through it."

"Yeah, I guess. I feel like all of my memories of you from that time are of, like, you and Jared and Trent laughing together at stupid shit."

"Are you really trying to call me the class clown? I mean, I know I'm cute, but come on...the class clown and the brooding beauty together? It's too much like a terrible romcom."

"Did you just say romcom?"

"It's a perfectly acceptable abbreviation. You didn't even notice that I just called you beautiful, did you?"

"Yes," I replied, smiling in spite of myself. He put an arm around me, and I tried to act cool. The last time anyone had put their arm around me, I was drunk. And the time before that. And the time before that. All of the times. Of course, all those times, the arm and whatever followed hadn't made me feel violated; just warm and sleepy from the drink. The violation came the next morning, when the arm around me had been replaced by self-hatred for not being able to carry on a normal relationship.

The fireworks began, and the view from the treehouse was perfect. Much like the parade, the fireworks had followed the same pattern for years. They were cut short that night by rain. For a while we sat there, in the treehouse, waiting for the drops to stop falling on the professional-grade roof and talking about nothing. Eventually we decided to make a run for it, and I was sitting in Tyler Hogue's garage apartment, which I will always call the garagepartment, trying to dry myself with a towel. I remember it, but I also remember feeling like I was watching myself from outside my body. I wasn't beautiful. I didn't run through the forest with a boy in the rain. She looked like me, but she wasn't me. He asked me if I wanted to stay. I did, but not as much as I wanted to avoid a conversation about it with my mother. More buzzy kisses were exchanged before the rain finally let up and the girl that looked like me began the walk home.

A few days later, I found Eduardo sitting on the patio as I left to go meet Lennie for a much needed update on each other's lives. I had been texting Tyler, I had a surplus of goodwill, and I decided to make another attempt at conversation.

"Did you go to the fireworks on the Fourth?" I asked. He shook his head no.

"I recorded them from here," he said.

"Explain to me again how you make your music. Like, when you compose something out of random sounds, how do you know what sounds good?"

"We're all human. We all know what sounds good."

"But not everyone likes the same music," I said.

"There are certain sounds that everybody likes," he said, "There are things we are biologically wired to do and like as humans that we cannot escape, but are always trying to redefine."

"What?"

"Monogamous relationships vs. multiple partners, greed, hunger, the inevitability of death. Feelings, mostly. People spend their whole lives trying to control their feelings rather than just letting them unfold. People spend years composing a 'good' song rather than allowing a song to simply happen."

Oh good, another hippie striving to live an authentic life among us mortals.

"Interesting," I said, for lack of more inspired words, "See you later."

I got in the car and drove a mile or so down the main road into Plodis, where there was a decrepit-looking Victorian house that someone had recently repainted and a sign out front made of old industrial gears welded together that read "buzz." The parking lot was an afterthought, the whole set-up seeming to cater much more to those who lived in cheap studios within a couple of blocks walk or who traveled by skateboard or bicycle. There was an odd concentration of young men outside carrying their skateboards, rather than actually using them for their intended purpose.

Much to the chagrin of the mustachioed barista, I ordered something brimming with sugar and commercialism and occupied a tiny table in the corner of what was once a living room, waiting for Lennie to get there. A mural on the wall, painted in arresting neon tones, had a tacky dashboard-type Jesus at its center, and the following words scrawled in acrylic paint around him: "Coffee Jesus can't save your soul...but a nice French roast can." I was still stuck on the skateboard carriers. I couldn't help but hate them for being such posers, but I suppose that is what we were all doing.

There was a common thread between all of us who were there, a sort of restlessness. No one was there because they needed more energy. The jitter we absorbed from the beans made us feel alive until we exhausted the thoughts rambling through our willing but neglected minds. Everyone there had the same level of professional discourtesy, the same amount of unoriginal thought, and the same lack of purpose, which they were trying to fix in this temple dedicated to rejecting one establishment and embracing another. The barista's laugh sounded like a donkey rearing. Do donkeys rear? I didn't think they did, but whatever, there wasn't supposed to be right or wrong here; just shades of ombre hair and drafts of "experimental fiction" that would never be published. The music playing in the background made me feel like I was at a circus. I felt guilty for making fun of the barista's laugh, though I was the only one who even knew I'd made fun of him. He had pretty blue eyes under that shaggy hair, and his mustache could be shaved, and maybe he'd make a nice companion while I ambled through life at a pace that afforded afternoons in coffee shops. At least he'd probably give decent head, sans mustache of course. I told myself to stop thinking about stupid shit, eat my four dollar scone, and revel in music about lost loves that I can only imagine was sung by some doe-eyed brunette in the type of dress that managed to make flowers look ugly. Feeling consummately lost and directionless, the thought of Eduardo's condescending attitude irritated me and I drummed my fingers against the formica table.

Lennie walked in fifteen minutes late in skinny jeans, biker boots, and thick black eye makeup. She looked much better suited to this place than I was, and the fact that she sounded like a smoker even though she'd never even had a cigarette gave her an edge with the barista, I thought. I was always a little jealous of her edginess and courage, if I'm honest. During college, her enthusiasm contagious, she made friends with everyone. She cheered convincingly at football games and was adept at charming hippies into giving her weed for free. Unlike me, she didn't really have dream worlds. If she wanted any part of something, she'd find a way to get it. This approach had left her damaged in her own way, but I was jealous of it all the same. She came over to the table and briskly set a mug on it before turning the vinyl-covered chair around and straddling it.

"So," she said huskily, "Tell me more about this boy. What's his name? Tyler?"

"What do you want to know?" I replied, clearly a cop-out.

"What does he look like?" I pulled up a picture of him on my phone. "Pretty!" she exclaimed. I smiled, another toothless, supposed-to smile.

"Is he rich?" she asked, "He's working at Daedalus, right? My friend Kimmie was dating a guy who worked there, and he bought her a Macbook for Christmas."

"I don't know," I said, "I'm not sold."

"Why not?"

"I don't know. Okay, I do know. I associate him with all the assholes I went to high school with, and I still feel like I'm the fat girl that doesn't get invited to dances."

"Addie, shut up. He obviously likes the way you look."

"He called me pretty at the fireworks and I felt like I couldn't trust him."

"Listen," Lennie said, "I know you're still reliving your teenage trauma, and I am sure that it sucked ass, but you need to snap out of it. This guy is cute, into you, and going to be really rich."

"Yeah," I said.

"What does your mom say?"

"I haven't really talked to her about it. Gran doesn't even know we've been spending time together and I already feel like she wants us to get married."

"Well, why don't you?" she said, with a tone of complete seriousness.

"Do you listen to yourself talk?" I asked.

"Well, he went to Yale. And your wedding would be an amazing party."

I acquiesced, before deftly turning the tables in her direction and asking to be updated on her life. She was still working at Purge and "feeling really good energy" about her relationship with hippie Brian.

"A couple more months and I can at least get my own apartment." she said, "I don't know, my life isn't that exciting. I just look at spreadsheets all day, then go home and eat ice cream until Brian gets off work."

"What kind of ice cream?" I asked.

"Does it really matter?" she replied, "How are the kids?"

"It's a pretty easy gig. I can't complain. Most nights I come home smelling like spoiled milk and just end up watching You-Tube videos."

"What YouTube videos?" she asked.

"Does it really matter?" I replied.

Our coffee drunk, we exited the shop and made empty promises to hang out more.

The life I wanted, it seemed, was more likely to be found at the end of a yellow brick road that began in Ravine, rather than amidst tacky art and multiple wearers of leg warmers. The mysterious dreamland of adulthood that I had been idolizing all those years was more easily accessed by driving a shiny new four-door sedan than by walking in the middle of the street with a dirty, old skateboard tucked beneath my arm. I hated that. I hated that I had to follow a yellow brick road and I already knew the ending. Even if I had bitchin' red shoes, I knew life here would eventually be a gross little man behind a curtain rather than a great and powerful wizard. It also seemed, though, that just like Dorothy, I had no choice but to move forward. Ravine wasn't perfect, but eventually I'd figure something out. Besides, I wanted the luxury of being horrified at the prospect of a hand-drawn, unlaminated sign commanding, "Bus your own dishes or die."

Sometime after the Fourth, Tyler left to go on vacation to Spain with his family, and I was back where I started, taking care of children and sparring with my mother. We had a quiet, sort of romantic night before he left. We were eating vanilla ice cream in the treehouse and I was trying to understand why a family with so much inner turmoil would spend two weeks together in enclosed spaces.

"Are you looking forward to it?" I asked.

He shrugged.

"Where exactly are you going?"

"Oh, all over the place," he said, "If we don't stay too long in one place, it's less likely that Mom and Dad will tear at each other."

"Will you have fun?"

"Sure. I mean we always stay at nice hotels and eat good food. Anyway, I feel like I should be there to keep the peace."

I squeezed his hand.

He continued, "You know my phone's not going to work over there, and I have no clue what my internet connection is going to be like."

"I'm sure I can manage without you for two weeks," I said.

"What about three?" he asked.

"Three might be a stretch," I replied.

We kissed, and I hated myself a little for being so nauseatingly flirtatious. Isn't that what every girl wants, though? Some boy who feeds her ice cream and teases her about wanting him while making it clear that he wants her? As I got ready to leave, he asked again what I was going to do without him. I said I'd probably sit at home and cry most of the time, before reminding him that I had to take care of the kids, all four of them, until camp started back up.

"You're so good with them," he smiled. I smiled back. I hated compliments, but he was looking at me like he might love me, and I thought for a second I might love him.

A couple of years before, I had submitted a poem I wrote to a literary journal and they'd sent me back some condescending bull-shit about not trying too hard to make sense out of life. With Tyler gone, and my dreams in full flight, I begrudgingly accepted that they might have been on to something after all. I had never thought that me in Ravine, dating a fellow Ravinite and being agreeable and domestic, would make an ounce of sense. Because I wanted so deeply to believe that I might never have to be alone again, that I might not have to rely on daydreams, I gave up whatever "sense" used to mean to me. Funny things happened when I gave up sense. I began wearing skirts and wedges because I wanted to, and stealing my mother's curling iron to add body to my hair, and baking elaborate desserts but not eating them. I wouldn't say I'd gone Stepford wife, but that seemed the only reasonable explana-tion when I found myself pulling the child-filled minivan into my parents' driveway to pick up Eduardo for a trip to the zoo. It had been my mother's idea, but because I was embracing nonsense, I was determined to win him over somehow, or at least not trauma-tize the children with his presence.

The Plodis Zoo was another cultural institution that had managed to remain open in spite of the city's falling fortunes. As a child, I had loved it mostly for the fact that it looked like the zoos that I had seen in picture books, rather than for its underwhelm-ing collection of animals. There were great stone posts and white wrought-iron fences and a beautiful old fountain and a man who sold perfectly spherical balloons and buttered popcorn. I hadn't expected Eduardo to engage at all with the children, but there he was, lifting Charlotte so she could see over the fence separating us from giraffes and answering her endless litany of questions not like a complete asshole. He read the plaque explaining why fish travel in schools to Alex and played peek-a-boo with Leo, who was overcome in adorable baby giggles. We stopped at a picnic table for lunch.

"I totally did not have you pegged as a kid person," I said.

"Why not?"

"I don't know."

"I've always wanted kids."

"But you've never come close?" I asked.

"I thought so once, but no."

"What do you mean?"

"I'm divorced."

"Oh, really? I mean, I'm sorry."

"Don't be sorry. It wasn't meant to be."

He tousled Leo's hair and looked away. I busied myself with making sure the other kids were eating. There was another dream world forming in which I could somehow convince Eduardo to take up the fold of happiness that I had yoked about my own neck. Bolstered by my new conviction that a little TLC would banish Eduardo's cynicism, I convinced him to come to Sunday dinner at Gran's. It all went fine until Gran accused him of being a communist. An awkward silence fell over the table, then Leo started crying, I couldn't stop laughing, and everybody made excuses about having to leave early. On the way out, Kaye asked me if I could give Darwin rides a couple times a week when she and George were busy. Nancy had been "singing my praises." I said yes, of course. There was no reason not to.

One morning the following week, I woke up unusually early. When my rumbling stomach wouldn't allow me to lie on my back and look at the sky through my window and tree branches anymore, I made my way to the kitchen. Mom was already sitting there, at the breakfast nook. It wouldn't have been so strange, except that usually she was reading the paper or picking at a dried out piece of toast, and today she was perfectly still, staring straight ahead. Looking back, I think she was jealous of what she perceived as growing closeness between Eduardo and I. Not on a conscious level, though. Her upbringing by two fairly self-involved individuals had left her, even years later, starved for attention. Anyone who unknowingly diverted it from her was a threat. Not even she recognized this, which, in turn, made her bouts of irritability seem random and undeserved.

"Hi," I said after a few moments.

"Hi," she replied tersely.

I began to get out ingredients for pancakes.

"Addie," she said in a whiny voice, "What are you doing?"

"Making pancakes," I replied, as if she couldn't see.

"I don't want to find a mess later," she admonished. I didn't say anything. Eduardo walked in, apparently to find some food, and her demeanor instantly changed.

"Good morning," she crowed, immediately engaging him in some asinine discussion of his work. I cracked the eggs.

"Christ, Addie," she said, "Don't break anything."

Seizing the rare opportunity that arose with a pause in Mom's rapid and uninterruptible stream of speech, Eduardo asked me what I was making.

"Pancakes," I replied, "Though I'm not sure if I can eat breakfast in the presence of a communist."

He laughed. My mother exhaled loudly. I started whisking the batter. I know I've already mentioned the tiresome little dream worlds I kept in my head, but this morning represented another layer of them. The clean, symmetric shelves contained a world where I wore business suits and ran half-marathons effortlessly next to a world where I pulled a Grace Kelly and married into royalty. There were also warped, mildewed shelves with cracked and dirty jars. Those jars were home to the world where I steered a hard left into the guardrail on the freeway just to see what would happen, and the world where I finally starved myself skinny so that my mother would have to focus on me and not her stupid resident artists. I ignored those jars, even as they anchored deeper into the muddy walls of my mind. I knew they were there and that acknowledging them would be helpful, but I pretended they were invisible.

"Mom, want a pancake?" I asked.

"No," she said.

"Eduardo?"

"No, thanks," he said.

After my pancake breakfast, I was a bullet in a gun, or more accurately, Augustus Gloop in the pipe of chocolate at Wonka. My mother was the pressure building up behind me, each sideways glance at me and drum of her fingernails on the table a sign that I needed to get out and get out soon. Not knowing where else to go, I walked to Gran and Pop's. They were somewhere on a beach in northern Michigan for a few weeks, thank God, and without thinking, I walked along the worn footpaths in the hallway rugs to the library. I envisioned the negative dream worlds building up in my head, cluttering my mind like expired groceries in the home of a hoarder. They would collect in piles underfoot and tumble out of forgotten cupboards until, at long last, I slipped on one of them and broke my neck. I found not exactly comfort, but the absence of abject nausea in running my fingertips across the spines of all the books, feeling canvas then leather, tracing a gold-embossed title. I opened one, a memoir of some kind. It had a sheet of tissue protecting the colored depiction of a family crest. They didn't make books like that anymore, I thought. There was another paper wedged in there, shiny and impossibly thin, with beautiful old script on it. I thought it must be some kind of joke, but I couldn't keep myself from opening it. It was in the same writing as that last nugget of wisdom that I had found and nearly forgotten, only this one said:

"It is difficult when your eyes automatically see another's soul. Reality, then, hardly seems exciting enough. Nothing is as profound as the unbroken and secret world contained within eyes.

Talk of the weather or the latest news does not rouse passion from the velvety chamber it has occupied, in this second world, this world of sparkling eyes and shiny souls. It is only in this dim and luxuriant un-reality, when I acknowledge the possibility of my future happiness, that I am left feeling content, but also wondering whether this empty cavity in my chest will ever become full of anything but passing wisps of aspiration. He looked at me and he cried, and I was not bothered. I realize I have never been afraid of achieving the extraordinary. It is the ordinary which terrifies me, the mundane which I find elusive."

I was crying. I never cried. I needed to escape again, to propel myself to somewhere less vulnerable, and I opened the French doors onto the terrace, thinking I would go for a walk in the woods. Kaye was already there, propped against a tree looking into the woods while her dog gallivanted on the lawn behind her back. It began to rain, but she didn't move, and as I walked home in the rain, relishing the way the wet cotton clung to my skin, I thought of how her heavy black eye makeup must be running down her face, creating a new road map over the natural one that had long since been botoxed away.

AUGUST

At the end of July, I had begun ferrying Darwin between the copious activities Kaye had cluttered his summer with and George's office at the University. Mid-afternoon, I would rescue Darwin from a grim cement building with signage that, while meant to evoke bright educational cheer, just made me sad.

"How was it today?" I asked.

"I hate it. I hate math," he replied.

"Yeah, I do too," I said, "I'm sure this will come in handy though. I always thought maybe I didn't like math because I just wasn't good at it."

"My teacher is arrogant and insufferable," he replied.

I'd never spent that much time talking to Darwin, but had soon come to realize that we were both misfits as far as Ravine was concerned. I could scarcely contain my delight when he A: expressed disdain for authority figures, and B: used vocabulary that the screener employed by Ravine Elementary School would have classified as advanced. Because significant crime had been committed in the vicinity of the University sometime in the past thirty years, my mother insisted that I be allowed to park temporarily in the gated parking area reserved for faculty that led straight into the building when leaving Darwin with George. George's lab had been built using some recent and exorbitant donation to the university by someone who hadn't actually gone there but was an avid supporter of the football team. It was shiny, and new, and improbably beautiful in its futuristic design. The interior was vast, an empty cavernous box, with an entirely glass ceiling through which the sun shone down on neatly organized groupings of plants and a bay of scientific analysis machinery that all looked as though it had come from an Ikea. George's office overlooked this cavernous room, and there would always be a couple of minutes in between our arrival and his emergence. I surreptitiously ran my fingertips across a tray of lush green grass, hoping that it wasn't being tested as a vector for disease, and soaking in the relative quiet that was there before propelling myself back into traffic.

Tyler should have arrived from Spain the night before, and I was sure he was sleepy and jet-lagged. However, at this point he'd had enough time to recover, so I called him as I drove home.

"Hello," he answered groggily.

"Hi," I replied, "How was Spain?"

"Spain was nice…"

"How was your family?"

"Tolerable…only one major blowout…"

"What are you up to?"

"Nothing."

"Well, what if I bring some food over and we can eat dinner?"

"Sounds good."

I put on a dress and stole one of my mother's frilly vintage aprons and went to the market Nan always went to, where you could buy a quarter pound of massaged kale and grass-fed steak that had been raised in a sunny pasture within twenty-five miles. I got us individual bottles of sparkling water and a slice of flourless chocolate cake. It cost a lot, but I wasn't worried, because the dream-world version of us where we lived in a red-brick walk-up with plants hanging in the window and wore effortlessly chic clothes and had the life that everyone wanted couldn't begin with Chips Ahoy and milk with hormones in it. No. Only flourless chocolate cake and fizzy water would do. He answered the door in pajamas with disheveled hair and almost involuntarily, said, "Wow." I walked in feeling smug, set my bag down, and put on my apron. Had I felt any more domestic, I might have given birth to a strapping baby boy right then and there. After making minor preparations, I tried, unsuccessfully, to turn on the oven. I walked over to the couch, where Tyler had parked himself and was on his laptop.

"Hey," I said, "Is there a secret to making the oven work?"

"Shit," he said, "It doesn't work. Sorry. I didn't even think about it. I'll make it up to you." I put the steak in the fridge, and he got up and started slicing nectarines, before pouring two bowls of cereal.

"Some men might give you cereal," he said, "and others might give you fruit, but only here could you get both. Full service."

I smiled. Normally I would have just been annoyed that all my careful shopping had been for nothing, but his incompetence in this situation was actually quite charming. Later, we lay in his bed, watching bad reality TV.

"Do you remember ninth grade English?" I asked.

"What about it?" he asked.

"Do you remember when I got into a fight with Ms. Smith about the meaning of a vocabulary word?"

"Was there just one time?" he asked.

"Well what about when I got into a fight with Carl Hunter?"

"Why don't you just tell me whatever it is you want me to remember."

"He was wearing a Howard Stern t-shirt, and I totally got into it with him about the fact that Howard Stern objectifies women and how he was perpetuating the patriarchy."

"Mm-hm."

"He spent the rest of the year convincing all the boys in the class that if they accidentally bumped into me in the hallways I would take legal action."

"That I remember," he interjected.

"Did you believe it?" I said, a little more accusatorially than I had meant to.

"I don't know, Addie," he said. He sounded annoyed.

"Well, tell me about Spain," I said.

"I saw an old couple on the street and thought of you."

"Why?"

"Because you'll be cute when you're old."

"Okay," I said, unsure of how I was supposed to react to such a statement, "Did you go to the Frank Gehry building in Bilbao?"

"The Guggenheim? Yeah, it was cool," he replied. He then proceeded to talk about something far less interesting, but it didn't matter. Maybe nothing mattered now, because I was there, I was finally the girl who cooked dinner and cuddled and was making someone think about forever. He asked if I wanted to stay, and I nodded my head. He had sliced a nectarine for me and he had run his fingers through my hair and that, to me, was everything a girl could want.

I don't remember the first time I had thought to myself that people couldn't be taken at face value, that they couldn't be trusted, but I hadn't ever been aware of feeling that way about myself until that summer. Before then, I had recognized my rich fantasy life as an escape, as a sort of "saving grace" against the harsh realities of my world. I didn't understand at the time Tyler's reluctance to talk about high school, but I began to have the sinking feeling that the judgment I had perceived from my hometown community throughout my childhood and adolescence was something I had fabricated in my head. I had hated everyone else for their inability to understand me, and during that time my life had been bereft of love and lots of happiness. Perhaps I should have buried my hatred and smiled. Perhaps I just didn't have a thick enough skin. Perhaps I needed to take a break from living in my head. The next day, after I had fallen asleep with visions of amazing architecture and international travel swirling in my head, I actually tried to parent the children, rather than shuffling them around and parking them in different places. I was determined, somehow, to spare them from the introspection I had been stricken with as a child. And, after I had put in a hard day's work (a.k.a four hours of mostly easy work) practicing social norms and expectations, I felt better.

In the Bible stories I had been made to read as a child, there was always something that made things worth it in the end. Noah builds his ark and doesn't drown in a flood. Abraham is willing to sacrifice his son and gains God's favor and the promise of immortality through descendants. Jesus doesn't yield to the devil, allows himself to be murdered, and saves the soul of everybody for all time. Ever since I had recognized how uncomfortable my unhappiness made people, I had really tried to believe that something like that was going to happen to me. I wanted there to be a payoff for the fact that I was acting carefree when I was anything but. I was in the library at the house again. Even with the yellowed cotton window sashes obscuring the outside world, something like sunlight was pouring in, and I fancied myself somehow lazily elegant as I brushed my fingertips across book spines and dislodged coatings of dust that had spent years accumulating. As was my habit, and, in part because I desperately needed some sort of biblical sign that I was on the right track and everything was going to be alright, I picked a book off the shelf and shook it, hoping some aged piece of paper would fall out with a wise message written on it. That didn't happen, and my eyes began to water a bit as I tore through an entire shelf, throwing books haphazardly on the writing desk until I saw a slip of paper flutter to the floor. Hands shaking, I read:

"I always thought that if I burrowed deep enough into my mind, if I prayed and hoped with all my heart, I might find a way to avoid time altogether. I haven't. I sat on the rocks today, by the water, and the morning glories were open, even though it wasn't morning. Little rebels, I love them so. Life should be effortless, but we weigh it down so heavily with tokens, and medals, and time. Perhaps the past is where these things, these odes to broken records, ought to stay, rusting in some case, nearly forgotten. The future holds with it the promise of new victories, new records broken. I am beginning to think that real victory lies not in having broken records, not in having been able, just for a second, to push past all the others, but in having broken all the rules."

The whole time I had known Lennie, we had bonded over our lack of serious relationship, over the phenomenon of not being wanted. From time to time, we'd both had entanglements, and we'd think for a second that the possibility of love existed. Usually, they just wanted to get in our pants. But we had stayed friends because we both knew what it was like when boys didn't even want sex. When they can neither love you nor objectify you, that's when it hurts the most. I thought of love and I wished for passion, but I also wished for safety, for someone who would place his hand against my collarbone, as if he had braked too fast at a red light and didn't trust the safety belt alone to keep me in my seat. When it comes down to it, there's a pretty subtle difference between the protective palm across the chest and the hungry, groping hand clutching at the breast directly below. But you cannot convince yourself that any kind of love or desire is there if the hand repulses at the suggestion of touching you. Lennie and I both knew what that felt like.

When she sent me a text saying that she'd gotten engaged to humanitarian Brian, I felt as though I'd lost an ally or something. I replied to her text with something along the lines of "Aw, girl, that is AMAZING! Congrats! Lunch soon :)" because I knew that I was supposed to be happy for her, and I was, kind of. I also felt slightly ill. I wasn't exactly jealous. After all, I had Tyler. I wasn't completely alone, so what did I care? The more pressing fact, the thing that I couldn't quite verbalize, but felt so acutely, was that I was sad for her days of dreaming to come to an end. Her getting married to this Brian character ruled out the crazy hypotheticals we had relayed to one another over bottles of cheap wine and shots of tequila. We'd both had plans to take the world by storm, somehow, to rise above the times we hadn't felt good enough and turn the tables on everyone. Her normal marriage ruled out the possibility that she would marry the president and use the Secret Service to prank the girls who'd been bitchy to us at a party. I knew it was ridiculous, but I couldn't shake the feeling that I had lost something. Even the sky that day looked unsure, like I thought the sky would look if there was a tornado. There wouldn't be. Sometimes they put the siren on and the wind would get scary and people would sit in their basements watching the doppler for a while, but nothing ever touched down. Because my feelings didn't make sense, and because the sky seemed as bizarre and unpredictable as my life was becoming, that day, I didn't walk home after work. I walked to Tyler's.

I wanted things to become predictable again. I wanted life to return to the murky, nothing-matters stage, where I had been able to feel happy. But marriage did matter. Tyler opened the door in a t-shirt and boxers.

"Hi," he said, "What's up?"

"I just got done watching the kids. I thought I'd stop by," I said as I walked inside. I sat on his bed and he followed me.

"What's going on?" he asked.

"Same old shit," I heard myself say, unable to make eye contact with him, because I was already trying so hard not to cry. He held me, without thought, it seemed, and wiped the tears from under my eyes.

"Talk to me," he said.

I shrugged. My feelings were enough of a burden for me. I couldn't begin to think of how to explain them to someone else. Because I couldn't think, I couldn't talk, and so I kissed. He kissed back. No one's reading this book to jerk off to (hopefully) and I'm not big on euphemism. We fucked. I got dressed and went home and lay in my bed just staring at the ceiling. After dreamily draining a bottle of wine I had brought from Gran's, I fell asleep with the overhead light on, not exactly happy, but thoughtless.

Everybody I counted myself close to had two first times. It was easy to lose one's physical virginity, especially if you drank enough. But then, there was the other time, the one where something much more vulnerable and fleshy and prone to bruising was exposed. The first time sex came with feelings attached, the game changed. That experience wasn't going to be easily replicated with another fifth of vodka and any warm, competent body. During the years that nothing mattered, in some dingy off-campus apartment, drunk and fumbling, and unromantically, I'd lost something. The event was precipitated by the fact that I had drunkenly followed Lennie and her boy of the evening home and then was there, an apparent obstacle to their satisfaction. He was the roommate who happened to be there and happened to start kissing me. We happened to have sex. I didn't orgasm. He was hospitable enough to offer me paper towels to wipe the cum off my stomach and a glass of water, but also reminded me that the whole thing had been "my idea", or I was at least "okay with it." It wasn't right. But it seemed easier to tell myself I'd enjoyed it and act like I could just add another line to my list of drunken mistakes than to admit to myself that I deserved better. Plan B was taken, and I tried to forget. Undoubtedly, my experience with Tyler had been much more positive, much more loving, but I felt numb all the same. I knew numb. I liked numb. Numb was what I needed in order to avoid regret or question.

Numb, I put on makeup in the morning and didn't think about the sociopolitical implications of doing so. Numb, I didn't have an inner dialogue that said "Oh, your eyeliner is really balancing out your double chin. At least if you're fat *and* in makeup, you can snag a chubby chaser." Numb, I drank my coffee without milk and sugar and didn't think "Wow, you're really cosmopolitan. At this rate, you'll be wearing power suits and firing people in no time." Numb, I held the baby and didn't hope against hope that his childhood would be easier than mine had been. Numb, I arranged for Lennie and her fiancé to meet Tyler and I for ice cream and didn't think, "Wait a minute. You don't do this country-club bullshit."

Tyler called at the last minute to cancel. He had to work late. He was really sorry. It was too late to call Lennie and reschedule, so I went anyway. When I got to the shop, Lennie was sitting at a table alone, chewing on the straw in her milkshake.

"Hey," I said, "Where's Brian?"

"Oh, he had some thing that he couldn't cancel. Where's your boy?"

"Working late, unfortunately. Let me see your ring! Tell me everything!"

"The diamond is certified conflict-free. He gave me this amazing speech about how I'm his soulmate and he never wants to live without me."

"Wow. So this is really happening, huh?"

She nodded, eyes brimming with happy tears. Fake smile

plastered on to my face, I sat there for the next hour talking. We both had things in our lives to be happy about. We laughed and talked about wedding color schemes and how well-endowed Tyler was. Full of ice cream and stuff normal people dreamed about, I had never felt more empty.

I came home to find Eduardo drinking beer and smoking on the patio.

"Do you know where my mother is?" I asked.

"I don't know, out somewhere I think," he replied.

"Can I have a beer?" He gestured affirmatively.

"Where are you coming from?" he said, staring across the patio as if in a trance.

"Oh, I was supposed to take my boy to meet my friend, but he couldn't go, so I just got ice cream with her."

"Sounds nice," he said, a smirk on his face.

"It was. Thank you," I said before taking a long swallow of beer.

"What does that mean, your boy?" he asked, "Is that like your boyfriend?"

"Not really," I said.

"Would he be mad if you started dating somebody else?" I paused.

"I guess so," I said.

"So basically your boyfriend." I drank my beer. He kept

talking, "Why did you want him to meet your friend?"

"What are you talking about?"

"Is it like some sort of test that he has to pass?"

"Not really."

"That's what it sounds like."

"So you've never introduced a girl to your friends to see if they think she's right for you?"

"I try to avoid relationships," he said.

"Why?" I asked, though I was nearly certain that I didn't want to know the answer.

"Humans are miserable creatures."

"Well," I said, "If you tell yourself humans are miserable, that's all they're ever going to be for you."

"They are miserable because they are miserable."

"Guess you'll have to stick to fucking goats," I said, stealing another beer and swiftly retreating inside.

SEPTEMBER

There's something that annoying people like Katherine Holt say of Ohio weather: if you don't like it, wait five minutes. I guess the point of that is to convey that the weather changes rapidly and is unpredictable. That's true. I'm more inclined to draw attention to the fact that Ohio weather is mostly dreadful and generally unlikeable in whatever form it takes. The only relief from manic variation between equally unpalatable extremes of blistering cold and sweltering heat are the months of March and September. Even in the years of my adolescent angst, I remember those months as times when Ravine seemed nice, and I wanted life to slow down, when mostly I just wished it would hurry the fuck up so I could get the hell out of there. That feeling of longing, the presence of weather that doesn't incite rage in the nicest of people, never lasts. There are far too many things that need to be done. Every March, when crocuses have started to bloom and the perfect breeze diffuses through the windowscreens, the end of the school year is fast approaching and banquets and ceremonies hang over the nice weather like rainclouds. Every September, when the leaves have started to change and the air conditioning can be turned off, school starts again and new outfits have to be bought, new lessons learned. So for every moment that year when I wished that time could just stop for a second, every wordless cuddle with Tyler and stroller ride with Leo, there was a corresponding reminder that time marched on whether I liked it or not. Gran and Pop were back at the house, returned from summer travels. Nan had allowed me to stay on watching Leo even though "she didn't really need it anymore," with the older kids in school. The me that wanted to take over the world chided myself for not accomplishing anything spectacular in my career, even if it had only been a couple of months since I'd graduated. But I began to think that maybe being a supportive wife and mother was my role in life, and maybe I'd just always been so scared of dependence on anyone else that I had automatically dismissed it as a possibility. I may not have been wearing a diamond and I wouldn't be getting a Mother's Day card, but goddammit if I wasn't comforting Tyler every night about how stressful his job was and reading Leo picture books over and over without complaint. Part of me was in love with the passivity of it all. Twenty-two years of constant thought, analysis, and contemplation had exhausted me. The drunken moments, the orgasm of unfiltered life that I'd found in between high school and the present made me believe that maybe I wouldn't have to be numb anymore. Maybe I could just be happy.

Tyler's abiding presence made me forget how much I hated myself, how much I hated the world, how much I had always wanted everything to be different than how it was. I remember the night I first realized how much I had trained myself not to expect love, how different it could have been. We were lying in his bed, dazed after sex, not talking about his job, not talking about my babysitting, not talking about how the future might unfold. He'd gotten up to go the bathroom and climbed back into bed, laying his head on my stomach and planting a soft kiss just north of my navel. It doesn't sound particularly romantic, and I doubt that he meant for it to be. I mean, it might have been sweet if I'd been pregnant, but praise Margaret Sanger, I was not. As much as domestic bliss was becoming more appealing, I was far from ready for an infant.

My belly was the first thing about my body I ever remember hating. Even before it was anywhere near a sign of obesity or diabetes risk, when it was a tiny, fleshy pouch on a nine-year-old pre-pubescent body, it made me "other." It was something that stuck out, that protruded, that prompted glances of disgust from my mother when I tried on new clothes, that broadcast to the world the fact that I had no self-control. I can't tell you how many times I had told myself that it didn't matter, that someone should love me for me, that society's standards of beauty were bullshit, that at least I had a pretty face. And I meant all those things when I told them to myself, but I told them to myself because I never heard them from others, because I was sure they were thinking, "God, just go to the gym," or didn't want to hear my childhood trauma. Nobody likes a complainer. But no matter how many times I told myself I was good enough, I never really felt good enough. Somewhere along the way there would have to be somebody else who came into the picture. Somebody who supplanted the memories of being the last kid picked in gym class with the thought that maybe, someday, you'd be the first pick in somebody's heart. That was the night when I finally stayed till morning. That was the night when I didn't immediately put clothes back on, when I let myself be held without feeling the impulse to recoil, when I fell asleep without analyzing the state of my life, when I didn't wake up before the sun.

I walked in the front door of my house the next morning in the burgundy wrap dress I'd worn the night before, wrinkled from its night on the floor, and went to the kitchen to take my pills. My mother was sitting there again, cup of coffee in front of her, staring into space. I offered a greeting, knowing that in so doing I was inviting dialogue. If I were smarter, I wouldn't have said anything.

"Where have you been?" she asked coldly.

"I was at Tyler's," I said, "I told you that's where I was going yesterday when I left." I got a glass and held it under the tap, waiting for the water to become cold enough to drink.

"Adelaide, I just don't think that's acceptable," she replied, "Think of your reputation."

"Are you serious?" I asked incredulously.

"Don't be juvenile," she replied, "I just don't want you to be surprised if people call you a whore."

The glass was overflowing onto my hand now, so I turned off the water and poured a little of it back into the sink. I was struggling to process her words. I knew that there was a darker layer of her personality, one that lay dormant most of the time, but usually showed itself in much subtler ways, and under the guise of loving concern. I turned to go upstairs.

"Addie," she said, "I just don't want to see you do something that you'll regret."

"I'm on the pill," I said flatly.

"Jesus, Addie, I didn't mean a pregnancy."

"What, then?"

"I don't know. I just don't want to see you get hurt."

"I'm an adult," I said, continuing toward the stairs.

"I won't tell your father," she said, in an oddly benevolent tone of voice.

"I don't give a fuck," I said, turning around again, "I'm twenty-two years old. Do I need to remind you that Palmer and Charles both lived with their girlfriends in college? Dad can deal with it."

"Addie, things are different for girls. Besides, do you and Tyler even call each other boyfriend and girlfriend?"

I was done talking. I stomped up the rest of the stairs, straight to the bathroom, and turned on the shower. She was right. Tyler and I didn't call each other girlfriend and boyfriend. But she didn't know what she was talking about. There were plenty of young people just like me who didn't have traditional relationships, and they were doing just fine. So what if I didn't call him my boyfriend. I hadn't been born after Women's Lib to deal with this bullshit. My rationalizations were true, but they didn't stop me from crying.

I emerged forty minutes later, in wet hair and yoga pants, and made a beeline for the couch, hoping that Mom would continue putting dishes away loudly and not try to come and talk to me. I fixed a steely gaze on the TV, ready to withhold, to act like I was impervious. I saw a shadow in the doorway and was surprised when I heard Eduardo's voice. He asked where something was in the kitchen and left again when I answered listlessly without making eye contact. I started watching an infomercial for some weird kitchen gadget. Images of brick-like muffins and meat that looked as if they had been wedged in a book press flashed across the screen. The machine looked like something that would be purchased and languish in a cabinet at Gran's house. Gran had, in her kitchen, an entire cupboard filled with cooking appliances that claimed to somehow improve lives. There was also a shelf with largely outdated fad diet books. Cabbage Soup, Grapefruit, Blood Type, you name it. I had once made the mistake of asking Gran about her collection. I say mistake because any discussion of food devolved into a discussion of how much life I would miss out on if I didn't lose weight. Of course, she credited her petite stature to her "composition" and "self-control." Eduardo was back.

"Hey," he said, "Can you help me with something?" Trying not to look bemused or annoyed, I asked what he needed help with.

"Come to the pool house," he said.

I followed him. I had had enough conflict for one day.

"I have to go to this function in Plodis, and I don't know what to wear," he said.

"Since when have you cared about how you look?" I blurted out, before backpedaling, "I mean, I didn't think you cared about what other people thought."

"Just help me," he said.

"Okay," I said, "What kind of event?"

"It's a dinner club for composers. There's this Plodis Music Society, and they have events for people that write music. What about this hat?"

He showed me a fedora that looked as though someone had sat on it for days. And just like that, I was crying again. He awkwardly patted me on the shoulder, and said, "Okay, okay, I won't wear the hat." I laugh-cried. He asked me if I wanted to talk about it. I shook my head, because I didn't know how to say that I felt guilty or out of line for accepting love that didn't come with some sort of hangover.

"Can I listen to your music?" I asked.

"If you want," he replied. I felt I had overstepped somehow.

"I don't have to, you know?"

"No," he said, "It's okay. You've been vulnerable in front of me. The least I can do is reciprocate."

I didn't like the sound of all of this vulnerability.

"Sit here." He motioned to a flattened grey recliner and offered me clunky headphones that made me think of the hearing screenings we'd done in elementary school, which is to say they looked like they had sat in a supply closet for a considerable number of years.

"Now," he said, "To listen to my music, you must close your eyes."

I obliged, but not before I had rolled them. I began to hear faint sputtering noises. There were, as I expected, sounds of cars turning on and off and other clanging guttural noises that I didn't recognize. It wasn't melodic. It didn't really sound like a song, or at least one that I had ever heard. But having my eyes closed, my ears flooded with unfamiliar sounds, and being perfectly still returned me to someplace where I had a chance at happiness. If I lived constantly drowning my thoughts in my senses, maybe I could live my life according to kisses on my belly rather than the social standards of my mother's childhood that I felt sure she hadn't followed but felt compelled to force on me nonetheless.

The song over, I opened my eyes to find him sitting directly across from me, his hazel eyes desperately searching for a tiny hint of recognition in every square millimeter of mine. I slid the headphones off my head and said, "I like it." A thin smile of relief crossed his face. I walked over to the closet and picked out a suitable outfit: fitted navy pants, a white oxford, a sweater without holes. Wordlessly, I hugged him. I hadn't expected him to be a good hugger, but he held on tight and for a moment, I felt safe enough to close my eyes. We had another silent moment of eye contact and tight-lipped smiles and I left, both calm and surprised by my calm.

When I walked into the beige disaster the next day to take care of Leo for a couple hours, I tried to make the situation less monotonous for both of us. Nancy had asked upon my arrival if I wouldn't mind straightening up a bit. But putting things back where they were supposed to go didn't seem to interest Leo, and it didn't interest me. Instead, I held Leo and spun in circles until we both collapsed in paroxysms of giggles on the beige carpet. I mean, I could have dusted about twenty shelves of books and cooked a grilled cheese and tomato soup lunch in the same amount of time, but the feeling of two tiny, soft hands on my cheeks and Leo's adorable baby laughter seemed more important. Much as I hated that my recent experiences sounded like narration from a bad made-for-TV movie, it was true. Trying to control my mother's opinion of me wasn't going to make me happy. But I could, for however short a time, be the one person in Leo's life who wasn't trying (whether they knew it or not) to slowly strangle the wonder from him, to little-league and advanced-class the quirkiness from him. My acceptance of his idiosyncrasies didn't exactly make it easier for him to blend in and survive. But figuring out normalcy didn't seem terribly important as Leo burrowed himself into a sort of blanketed nest next to me on the couch, smiling at me for no reason. Nan came home.

"Didn't get a chance to clean, huh?" she said in a mildly irritated tone of voice.

"We were too busy dancing, right, Leo?" I said, pointedly avoiding eye contact with the harried woman in the corner. He had somehow become upside down, but I thought I detected a head nod.

"Okay," Nan said with a sigh, "Here's your money. Can you drop this casserole dish by the house? I told Crisp I'd get it back to her by tomorrow."

"Okay," I said. I kissed Leo on the forehead and left, trying not to read anything into the fact that his doe eyes followed my every step out the door. It wasn't that big of a deal, dropping off a casserole dish, but I wondered why Nan hadn't just done it while she was out and about, and whether it had only become my job because I had cared for her child instead of cleaning her house. Gran opened the door, looking confused. I held up the casserole dish.

"Nan asked if I would bring this by," I said.

"Come on in," she said, "How's that going? I mean the kids. How are they?"

"Good," I said, following her into the kitchen, "You know I just have Leo now."

"Mm," she said, "Something to drink?"

"No, thanks. I shouldn't stay too long."

"Still seeing the Hogue boy?"

"Yeah," I said, "But he's out of town for work for a few days."

"Such a handsome boy," she said.

I nodded. The phone rang, and she answered it. I motioned to her that I was going to the library. Whatever inner conflicts I had could be silenced by the discovery of another thin slip of antiqued writing. I tried to remember where I had found the last mysterious paper. I wondered whether there was some secret pattern to their placement that I hadn't figured out. I pulled a couple of books from the shelf and gently shook them to see if anything would come loose. I felt a little silly that I was afraid of what would happen if Gran popped in at any moment and caught me snooping.

The antique furniture and framed prints of wildlife on the wall seemed meant to enforce my family pride while reminding me that if I pushed too hard I might break something. I closed my eyes and pulled a book from the shelf, tempting fate and slipping it quickly into the tote I was carrying. Gran was deeply engrossed in conversation, so I left, my nosiness undetected in the end. I went home and forgot about the book in my zeal to take care of the things I needed to do. I painted my nails in front of the television furtively, so Mom wouldn't freak out about the possibility of a stray drop ruining the carpet. I answered a series of wedding-related texts from Lennie. Were calla lilies overdone? I didn't know. I had dinner with Mom and Dad; some sort of chicken. Lean protein.

"Are you still looking for job?" Dad asked.

"I have a job," I said.

"Come on, Addie. You know what I mean."

"Not really," I said, "And I'd appreciate a little less pressure from you about it."

"Now, Addie," my mother said, "You know this is just because we care about you. We don't want you to have to struggle like Charles."

Charles is my middle brother, a defector from the family empire. He was "struggling" because he had chosen to squander his valuable education on work that was unrelated to finance. He had met his girlfriend, a militant vegan who didn't shave her legs, during his time in the Peace Corps, and was now working at some ethical, small-batch coffee roaster on the West Coast.

"Well," I said, "First of all, I am not Charles. Second of all, how is Charles struggling?"

"No health insurance, no IRA," my father said, "Listen, kid, you don't want to be in that situation."

"Alright, alright. Just settle down," I said, bracing myself for the fact that this conversation would be repeated at every meal I had with them until I had assuaged their fears.

Having narrowly escaped an extension of the job conversation, I took a shower, lay in bed, and waited for Tyler to call from whatever backwater town he was in pitching mutual funds to a teachers' union.

"Hi," I said.

"Hey, Beautiful." I smiled and walked over to make sure the door of my room was completely closed.

"How's the trip?" I asked.

"It's okay," he said, "kind of in the middle of nowhere, but I guess that's what you do when you're the low man on the totem pole."

"Yeah," I said, "Any takers for your thing?"

"Nah, they won't make the decision until after I'm back home. How's Leo?"

"He's adorable," I said, "We spent like an hour just spinning in circles until we fell down today."

"They're lucky to have you."

"I don't know," I said, "I think Nan was pissed that I didn't spend more time cleaning."

"Well, that sounds like bullshit. Anyway, I'm glad to have you."

"Oh, you have me now, do you?"

"Settle down," he said, "We're far past the point where you can sue me for calling you pretty."

"Shut up," I said.

"I can hear you smiling through the phone," he said, "is it safe to say that you're happy to have me too?"

"I don't know if it's safe, but you could say that."

"I should go to bed," he said, "I've got an early morning tomorrow. Sleep well."

"Sweet dreams," I said, hanging up the phone.

I wanted to fall asleep, then and there, in a cloud made of good dreams, but the fact that my heart was on the ceiling wasn't going to allow for that. Maybe I should actually try to read the book I'd taken from Gran's. It was impossibly dry, some romance from the era when ankles were risqué, but I felt compelled to make myself continue, wanting to be worthy of the esteem Tyler had just expressed toward me. I almost didn't catch that there was another letter in between the pages. The paper was so thin, like pages in a Bible, almost transparent. But there it was, waiting for my eyes to hungrily devour it.

"I always knew that I would be a mother someday. It was

a foregone conclusion, more than a decision I ever had the power to make. My abdomen used to be a place that reminded me I was alive. My lungs would breathe and I could move about as I pleased. My stomach would gurgle and I could eat mulberries. My heart would beat, rhythmically, slower and faster and I could know, simply by its beating, when I was afraid, elated, or exhausted. With a baby growing inside me, there is plenty to distract me from who I am beneath it all. When the baby comes out, I will once again become a hollow tree, whose sole concern is my own survival. For now, I am a hulled human that has been stuffed full of others' secrets, their joys, and their fears. I am not solid and strong. I am an empty vessel who will come perilously close to death in order for others to live. I tell myself that this is not wasted. The life of my own has been cleared away, yes, but it nourishes those around me, mixing with them so that I am never really lost. And anyway, maybe there is something to transferring what life I have to others. Maybe if I keep giving birth to others, my breath will become faint enough to ferry me past mere survival, and on toward heaven."

I didn't really know what to make of it, except for the fact that I could derive value in my life from nurturing others, which I already knew. Not my family. I had issues with most of them, except Leo. And not people like Eduardo, who, though he had behaved almost like a human once or twice, still seemed too preoccupied with his own trauma. Tyler was the only person I could think of who returned my compassion in a way that wasn't biting or slightly underhanded. I thought of the view from Gran's library that I imagined as the backdrop for the writing of these strange epistles. The river. The trees. Back when he had first arrived, Eduardo had made some artsy pronouncement about the scene, as if there were some social commentary to be gained from the riparian barrier between Ravine and Plodis.

"It's always been that way," I'd said.

My primary objective was to shut him up. But I was just as intent on telling myself that things in Ravine, probably the world over, gave a thought to changing every once in a while, to moving outside the natural boundaries that had been set. Just as easily as that thought entered the collective consciousness, it was dismissed. It was easier to get a job you hated that offered insurance to cover anti-depressants than to constantly explain your feelings to people who had no stake in understanding them. It was easier to accept what love was given to you than to argue about why love wasn't distributed evenly.

"Always doesn't exist," Eduardo had replied.

OCTOBER

My parents' constant inquiries into the state of my employment necessitated some sort of action. So, I began volunteering at the conservatory in George's lab and feeding Mom and Dad some bullshit about how I was going to apply political theory to botany to get into graduate school. It wasn't intellectually stimulating, but there was something methodical and enjoyable about misting plants and measuring the lengths of their stems. I tried very hard to think that if I approached my entire life this methodically, I might enjoy that too. Every negative emotion, I decided, was a result of this strain between where I thought or had been told success lived and where I was. I at least no longer looked as though I were dying a slow and excruciating death, as I had between the ages of eight and eighteen. Back then, sometimes I had tried to smile. But mostly I was chided for sighing audibly in class and rolling my eyes. I was now to the point where, Prozac in my bloodstream, I could smile without effort, but I found solace in the conservatory, because the plants didn't care whether I was cheerful or not.

Outside, the city began settling into fall, cold and damp when the sun wasn't shining. The conservatory was always awash in abundant rays of artificial light and piped full of warm, humid air. My parking privileges revoked for longer-term stays, I had to walk through a dusty brick building with lead-paned windows, probably the original botany building, and down a dark hallway with storage rooms on either side. The newer conservatory was like some sort of weird, cyborg skin graft on this crumbling hive of old classrooms. There was a sort of comfort, though, in the gradual journey from dark to light, from past to future. The quiet was normally overwhelming in comparison to the rest of the bustling campus, but on a particularly damp day that October I heard raised voices coming from behind one of the heavy wooden doors. It took me a second to recognize them as those of George and Kaye. I couldn't make out full sentences, but it didn't sound like a happy exchange. They were an odd couple, to be sure, but I had never sensed any serious discord. Then again, I thought, I described my parents as happily married when they had just developed highly specialized ways of avoiding each other.

Kaye had married George after having him as a professor. He didn't seem to care about much besides his plants and wore years-old blazers that never quite fit. Their division of labor was very clearly defined. She had social skills and he had intellect and the material comforts his intellect afforded. Her rebellion against Ravine did have its limits. She may have married her teacher, but he also ensured that her nail polish, though black, was $40 a bottle. Her e-cigarette, though frowned upon, was the same brand as Leonardo DiCaprio's. I thought I could hear footsteps so I quickly moved on to the conservatory, touching my ID card to the reader that made the glass doors hiss open like some sort of spaceship. I saw both of them walk past the doors and toward the exit and I felt relieved not to have been detected. I made my way through the labyrinth of plants, misting and trying to let my mind go blank.

Upon their return, I was quickly spotted and they came over to see me. Kaye was holding a Diet Coke and looked quite cold even though she was wearing a wool trench coat. George followed in his usual wrinkled and professorial garb.

"Addie," Kaye said, "It's so awesome that you're volunteering."

"Yeah," I replied, "It's been a really nice break from babysitting."

She smiled, "Oh, yeah, the kids are back in school, right?"

"Yeah," I said, "It's just Leo. Where are you guys coming from?"

"Oh, I just stopped by to take George out for some lunch."

"Where at?"

"There's a greasy little diner over on Third that we used to go to all the time when we first met: Maxine's"

"What did you get?"

"A salad with grilled chicken."

"Yum."

"Mm-hmm."

At this point, George made some comment about having to get back to work. They gave each other a thoughtless peck and he went back to his office. Kaye and her short fingernails, which looked severe with all the bulky rings she wore, stayed to half-heartedly examine various plants.

"Kind of stuffy in here, huh?" she asked. I nodded.

"Hey, while I have you here," she said, "I have a favor to ask. Mother's been given the old heave-ho for the Harvest Festival, but that means that I have to do it. Would you be at all interested in helping me do random prep at the house? I mean, I know it's not exactly a glamorous job, but we can have wine or something."

"Sure," I said, feeling that perhaps Kaye could help me figure out how Ravine would fit into my future.

"Great. You're still good picking up Darwin on Thursdays?"

"Yep."

"Okay, Addie. I'll text you."

And just like that, among trays of pansies and tabletops of sod, I had committed myself to another helpful role that would get me no closer to gainful employment.

The Harvest Festival, like the Independence Day celebration, was another hallowed Ravine tradition that had hardly changed since its inception. It was more or less a glorified Halloween Party, but the moniker of Harvest Festival distanced it appropriately from Satan. Held at City Park, it featured apple cider and cinnamon-dusted doughnuts and "fun activities for all ages." Face painting, decorating baked goods in seasonal sprinkles, and wagon rides through a "haunted" forest. Like most community events in Ravine, it was best loved by individuals under the age of ten. Given Ravine's baby-factory status, it was a popular occasion. It was one of those things that everybody loved to come to and nobody wanted to organize, which of course meant that Gran had kept it afloat for years by twisting people's arms into participating. It seemed she had finally tired of busting heads over seasonal crafts and heaped the responsibility onto Kaye's shoulders.

When I told Tyler that I had been tapped to participate in this tradition, I swear his smile grew three sizes.

"Mom used to help with that," he said, "I'll be damned. You're turning into Holly Homemaker before my very eyes."

"I'll sue you for calling me that," I joked, with a hint of seriousness. While I wasn't against having a somewhat domestic persona, and was even embracing it to some degree, I was getting traces of Norman Bates. I found myself wondering if I put on one of his mother's aprons and nothing else, just how big of a boner he would get. When I said this to Lennie, she told me I was overreacting, and besides I had to stay with him till Halloween because couples costumes were the most fun.

In the back of my mind, I wondered when I would reach the right balance, the crux of happy, and once I was there, was I finally going to be satisfied, or were my expectations going to change? I wanted to get myself so un-screwed-up that the elusive world that operated on happiness in belonging would be available to me. In that sense, my only hope was to fill my time with distinct roles and finite possibilities. Harvest Festival it was. The thoughts didn't stop.

I was fifteen the first time I was prescribed Prozac. I've been on it ever since, give or take a few milligrams. It had helped, in terms of not being bitchy to strangers and not having a constant inner monologue running, but it clearly hadn't kept me immune to the existential crises of young adulthood. Regurgitating my childhood traumas to another therapist didn't seem as though it was going to make my confusion dissipate, either. At school, I had had plenty of homework and other people's petty drama to distract me from the future. And, of course, if I got particularly desperate for release, I had long-islands and "dancing." Lately, in the absence of both of those things, the easiest form of distraction was fucking Tyler. That sounds callous, I guess, as though I was using him. He was great for other things, too, obviously. We watched old movies, took long walks, and had engaging conversation about policy and economics. But anything that wasn't sex forced me to think about the future, about being cast in a role that I wasn't ready for or being dismissed from the production altogether. Of course, I liked the idea of sharing something unique with another person. I didn't know, though. A collection of harvest festivals and conversations about whether to bring wine or flowers to a dinner party was not exactly the unique that I wanted. Sex was the only way that I had found to remind Tyler of who I was absolutely not going to be (a chaste housewife in a marriage that had produced a kickass treehouse and beautiful children but not much else), while keeping myself from thinking about the fact that I had no idea who I was actually going to be. Besides, it had long been my belief that an orgasm a day keeps the doctor away.

Though Gran had officially relinquished her role as grand marshall of the Harvest Festival, she wasn't great with ceding control in any situation, and so she was insisting (kindly offering, if you asked her) that Kaye use the library at the house as a sort of war room, where pumpkin appliqués could be hot glued onto all manner of things and menacing phone calls compelling people to stand in the woods and scare small children for four hours could be made. I showed up for my first day of servitude to find Gran opening the door of the house with one of her rotary telephones glued to her ear. Gran and Pop had never quite cottoned to the idea of cordless phones, such that each rotary phone in their house was attached to an unnecessarily long and stretchy coiled cord. It was an acquired skill to dodge them, especially if Gran and Pop were both on the phone at once, talking into different units. I bobbed and weaved through this obstacle and found Kaye in the library, her shock of artificially platinum hair bent over complicated-looking charts that she appeared to be highlighting in about six different colors.

"Hey," she said, looking up after a couple of seconds.

"Hey," I said, "How's it going?"

"Oh, alright," she said, "I mean it's not what I would spend my afternoon doing voluntarily, but you know…"

I laughed, "How can I help?"

"Can you alphabetize that stack of papers, please? They're Gran's files on people who've helped out in the past."

I went over to the writing desk and began leafing through yellowed pieces of paper, all of which had a name at the top and various clusters of sentences written in different shades of fountain pen ink.

"Thanks for helping with this," Kaye said, "If I had to spend hours in an enclosed space with most of the women in this town, blood would be shed."

"Has Gran kept these records the whole time she's been in charge of the festival?" I asked.

"I think so," Kaye said, "Some of the names in there are people who are dead. It's pretty fucked."

I read a sampling:

Her arms are evidently too fat to craft good center pieces.

Whining about having to wear a shapeless ghost costume, as if the children need to see her implants.

"So high school," I said aloud without exactly meaning to.

"Yep," Kaye said.

"Why did you ever come back here?" I asked.

"I realized how important family was to me," she said, "and New York got to be too much."

"Oh, yeah. I always forget that you lived there. When was

that?"

"The late eighties," she said, "There's not much to know."

"Still," I said, "I feel like you're the only one who ever actually intended to get out."

She smiled. "Well, I don't know," she said, "I guess everybody dreams about getting away when they're young."

"You modeled, right?"

"Well, yeah. I graduated high school a year early and moved to the city and picked up modeling while I was supposed to be in school for fine art."

"Sounds very glamorous…"

"It was a lot of fun for a while, but the industry was toxic. I failed out of school and moved in with a photographer."

"Whoa. What did Gran say?"

"I didn't tell her. I mean, they didn't know until the school notified them. It's not like they approved, but they never approved. They tolerated it when I got a show at a gallery…you know, something mildly impressive. But, without education, they were convinced I was going to end up homeless."

"Sounds about right. Did you go back to school?"

"Yeah, I went to State for a couple of years when I moved back. That's where George and I met."

"But, if you were selling art, why did you ever leave New York? I mean, faults and all, it has to be more exciting than Plodis."

"You've evidently never heard the story of my blot on the family tree."

I looked at her quizzically.

"Oh, it's nothing really," she said and looked away. I could never figure out how to react to her words. One-on-one, she had about her a certain melancholy that could have hinted at something sad just as easily as something beautiful. I couldn't make out whether the moisture in her eyes was a happy sparkle or the beginning of tears. While the next logical clue to look to would be the tone and variation of her voice, this did not help at all. Each word was spoken with an even coolness, as though she was reciting a list of miscellany that had nothing to do with anything else. I imagined the bursts of passion that should have been assigned to syllables of speech rising like great lumps in her throat only to recede slowly and sluggishly into whatever dark cavern they had emerged from. I hadn't looked away from her since her mysterious dismissal, and she began to speak again.

"Oh, it was the eighties. Cocaine was everywhere."

"You did cocaine?" I asked.

"Yeah," she said, looking away, "The guy I was living with, too, and then he moved on to heroin and things got kind of bad. So your grandparents came and carted me off to rehab."

"Oh my God."

"Well, you know how it goes in Ravine. Chances are if you're not at college on some sort of scholarship, you're developing a chemical dependency. Don't tell your Dad I told you. He expressly forbid that when you were born."

"I won't," I said, "You know Dad. Next time I got a speeding ticket, he'd blame it on your wayward influence."

She laughed nervously, "Shit! What time is it?"

"Three," I said.

"Fuck. I have to change clothes and go pick up Dar from school. We're having family portraits taken today. If we don't get them done in fucking October, we won't be able to get them printed into Christmas cards in time. Same time in a couple days?"

I nodded. She slung a giant leather tote over her shoulder and rushed from the room.

I finished alphabetizing the files that Gran had created, wondering if she hadn't suggested her house as a workspace solely to ensure that none of her insane judgments risked exposure to the public. Well, I thought, if Kaye can find a happy place in Ravine, especially after having been someplace much more exciting, maybe I can too. But there I was, thinking again, and hadn't I endeavored to stop doing that? I went over to the bookshelves, pregnant with ideas about how to comprehend my own future through someone else's fiction.

From the point of my baptism, as an infant, I had been taught to look for salvation between the pages of books. To search for answers in text, to read between the lines. But, I was also a student of methodology and efficiency, things I suppose I had my father to thank for. In elementary school, I thought myself clever for tackling word searches not at random, but line by line, left to right. I would just have to apply my fifth-grade logic to the entire library if I wanted to be sure I had found every last drop of wisdom it contained. I started in one corner, removing each book from its shelf individually and rustling the pages, handling each one as though it might contain my holy grail. I drew my fingertips across each texture, somehow gaining peace from brushed canvas, or finding God by retracing the gold-embossed title, the messiah on each delicate page I turned. The first set of shelves yielded two letters, which I stashed in my purse without reading. I had just begun combing the second shelf when Gran came in.

"I didn't know you were still here," she said, almost accusatorially, "Kaye left an hour ago."

"Oh, yeah," I said, "They're taking family portraits."

"Mm," she grunted, "And what are you up to?"

"Oh, I should go too. I'm supposed to get dinner with Tyler."

Her expression changed from possible annoyance to a smug smile. My behavior didn't matter if I attached myself to a man.

I went home and read the two letters I had found, one after the other.

"It is nearly Christmas, and clad in shapeless dresses, a swollen belly in front of me, I can do little more than aimlessly pace up and down the corridor, wearing the carpets thin and leaving crescent moons on all the tables that fall victim to my drumming fingernails. I feel guilty for the faith that is leaking from me, and I want desperately to be happy, but I cannot figure out how. I opened the library doors today, and walked across the hard, dead grass in the meadow wearing only the velvet dress that hung over my frame like a too-big pie crust. I found myself kneeling at the river bank, eyes blurry with tears, lacquered fingernails clawing feverishly at the ice, trying to reach water that was moving, to access faith that would tell me life doesn't completely freeze, it doesn't lose all ability to change. I stopped and went back inside before anyone noticed I had gone. Is there really any difference between seeking faith and seeking escape? We hope that faith will give us deliverance, and what is deliverance but a form of escape? I have always thought my deliverance must lie in movement toward a purer faith. Perhaps I am wrong. Perhaps deliverance is escape."

Then:

"Papa used to say that he came here from Bavaria to make a better life for himself, for all of us. He said he didn't want to be a king, he only wanted to be a man. Kings had too much wealth - they could be ruthless, exacting, cold. Adriel is no king, but he is all of those things, all of the qualities that are excused when clothed in gold. These shortcomings didn't matter so much to Papa, because, you see, kings also live in the finest castles, eat the best food, wear jewels, and have beautiful women. If I married Adriel, I would have all of these things, and I guess they were meant to be enough. Listening to the light opera and wearing satin slippers is all very well, but these niceties are, one after the other, covered in some sort of wax. It is dull, easily broken with the well-placed tip of a fingernail. These things will never keep my mind from wanting to know where the water in the river rushes to. I feel like a statue with its feet stuck in cement, only my cement is this wax, this preservative that accumulates as fast as it is wiped away. Each day brings some bad weather, something that makes me wish I could lift my feet from the pedestal. But I am too heavy, and the wax, though weak in small portions, is too strong when pooled around my feet. I will have to wait until He carves the extra weight from me. Then, perhaps, I will be light enough to fly away."

There seemed to be initials on the bottom of this one: HW. I didn't recognize them. There was a family tree in a drawer in the library, and I couldn't remember any H names, but I would have to leave that for another time. Words can say whatever you need them to, and all I could read into this situation was that my family, my past unhappinesses held me back, and Tyler was maybe someone who could free me. If I didn't throw myself headfirst into whatever it was Tyler and I had, I would be forever wondering what real life felt like. So, preparing for dinner, I put on a dress and makeup and sprayed perfume on myself, looking how I thought I must, I guess, to make life together a lasting venture, or at least to banish thoughts for half an hour. Tyler had said he would call after his extended work happy hour was finished. I felt silly for being proud, in a way, that I was the reward for having had to sit with red-faced men in greasy-looking suits as they traded stories about vacations to all-inclusive resorts and the rising cost of their favorite cufflinks. I went downstairs, where my mother said I looked pretty and I wondered whether she meant it and whether I could ever reach the place where I didn't care if she meant it. She went back to the TV room, where she was watching something depressingly uplifting with my father. I went, with a glass of water, to the patio, waiting for a text, a call, a summons, a show of love. It didn't come, it didn't come, and then the blue light from my phone lit up the dark and I felt relieved.

"Hey," he said, "Sorry, but I'm going to have beg off for tonight."

"Are you at the happy hour?" I asked.

"I'm on my way home," he said, "There's a surprise meeting at like 8 a.m. tomorrow in Cleveland, and I'm gonna have to get up stupid early."

"Okay," I heard myself say, "Sweet dreams."

"Thanks, Babe," he said before the phone clicked off. I remained seated, sedentary as the phone once again went dark, plunged into the semi-darkness that only the dull incandescence of suburbia can provide, disheartened and annoyed. Minutes later, Eduardo emerged from the pool house, looking unsettlingly dapper, almost as though he'd been dipped in some sort of Ravine solution. He was wearing a bow tie for fuck's sake.

"Where are you off to?" I asked.

"Plodis," he said, "Some new gallery. And you?"

"Nowhere."

"You telling me that you're all gussied up for nothing?"

"Jesus, did you just say 'gussied up'? You sound like you're from hill country. I was supposed to hang out with Tyler, but something at work came up."

"You wanna come to the gallery?"

"No, no, that's okay," I said.

"Don't be silly," he said, "Come on. I don't want to go by myself anyway."

I walked after him, nothing to lose. He went toward the end of the driveway and I realized he intended to take the bus.

"I can drive," I said, and just like that, I was driving my car into Plodis, a bow tied Argentinean at my side. The alternative arts scene in Plodis couldn't quite rival that of Brooklyn or Silver Lake, but it tried, oh, how it tried. As an Ohioan, it goes without saying that an infinitesimal percentage of my consciousness is automatically funneled into coastal rage. It's not that New York and Los Angeles aren't cool, or whatever, but living in a closet for a small fortune just doesn't make up for the fact that there's dog shit in the middle of the sidewalks and people who "pig out" on fat-free frozen yogurt. My confusion at Eduardo's attendance of any sort of celebration aside, we entered a storefront in the factory district, exposed brick and all. I know art is subjective, but I honestly could not get over the exceptionally poor quality of work on display. Choices for purchase were limited. There were depictions of evil Disney characters that looked like someone trying to get rid of their old tempera paint had emptied it onto canvases and covered it with jagged pieces of faux velvet. There were paintings that, while they had technical skill, depicted things like mermaids and fauns. I tried to imagine these artworks on living room walls or overlooking bustling family dinners, but I couldn't. I wanted to pile them up, spray them with butane, and light a match. I couldn't do that either.

Then there were the people. Some girl who looked exactly like Boy George circa 1985 was doing a lopsided two-step in the corner. A white man with dreads who kept drinking whatever remained in glasses that people had set down on the "found" tables tried to discuss the art with me. I had chosen to come, I told myself. It was my fault that I hadn't considered the serious ramifications of accepting cultural guidance from Eduardo. He was busy lurking at the fringes of the crowd, surreptitiously producing a handheld recorder and capturing sounds. I was trying desperately to look interested in *Minnie Mouse & Meat Cleaver # 1* when he snuck up behind me and muttered something about this being the most culturally significant event he had ever attended. I turned, ready to lambaste him for saying such a thing. He was grinning. Oh my God. He was joking. He remained silent as I burst out laughing, producing his recorder and clicking it off.

"Oh, come on," I implored.

"Come on, you want to leave? I agree," he replied cheekily. Both happy and annoyed I followed him out of this lair of disturbing images. We wandered into a pizza place a few doors down and over greasy slices of plain cheese on paper plates, he asked me what I thought. "Interesting" seemed the kindest response, and the one easiest to convey while struggling with stringy mozzarella.

"Well, I thought it was shit," he said.

"That's another way to put it," I laughed, "Still, I guess you've got to give people credit for putting themselves out there."

"No," he said, "I don't."

"You were doing so well," I said, "getting dressed up, leaving the pool house."

"No, I won't give them an ounce of credit," he said, "Art things like that are always so contrived. So full of people just pretending to be things they are not."

"How do you know they're pretending?" I asked.

"Because I used to be one of them," he said, "When I was married my wife was an artist and we had to go to things like that all the time. I was even more annoying about my work then, if you believe it."

I smiled. "What happened? With your marriage, I mean?"

"She ran away with another man," he said, trying very hard not to look heartbroken.

"I'm sorry," I said.

He shook his head as if to signal that it wasn't a big deal.

"Ready to go?" he asked. I nodded. We drove home in silence. The more time passed, the more difficult it became to think of anything to say to break the stalemate. Home, in the driveway, I intercepted him for a hug.

"Hey," I said, "Thanks for getting me out tonight."

"My pleasure," he softly replied. I pulled back and our eyes locked. Neither of us looked away, and I stood transfixed by those eyes that seemed always to be searching for something beneath the surface. He leaned forward, as if to kiss me and I wanted nothing more to abandon thought and revel in the momentary anesthesia of a kiss. But I thought of Tyler, broke the hug, and rushed inside.

A couple of days later, when Tyler had expressed appropriate remorse for his last-minute cancellation, and I had recovered from my art-nouveaupocalypse, we were lying in bed and he was nuzzling the back of my neck and I was certain that being more content was simply impossible.

"My mother keeps asking me if we're dating," he said sleepily and close enough to my ear that I could feel the moisture in his breath.

"What do you tell her?" I replied in similar fatigued tone, though my heart was racing.

"I tell her I don't know," he said.

"You don't?" I asked. He turned me over so that we were face to face, a look both of adoration and annoyance on his face.

"That's enough from you," he said, before kissing me.

"Well, you're the one who brought it up," I said.

"I mean, I do feel a warmth for you…" he said.

"Great," I said. What I wanted to say was "That's great, because your dick seems to feel something for me as well." Evidently, my facial expression spoke for itself. I couldn't be held responsible for that, surely.

"I don't know," he continued, "I'm just weird about relationships. But I guess that's basically what's happening, right?"

"Listen," I said, "My threshold age for marriage is thirty, so if that's freaking you out, it shouldn't. As long as we're both happy, I don't care. Although, you should know that Lennie does call you my boy because she doesn't know how else to refer to you."

"Oh, Jesus," he said, "Well, I suppose that's good enough."

I was a naturally inquisitive child. Rather than leaving anything well enough alone, I would snoop for previously undiscovered treasures in places I wasn't allowed. These discoveries could be as simple as finding a bag of chocolate chips that Mom had pushed to the back of a pantry shelf and tried to cover with egg noodles, or finding some horrendous velvet creation from an eighties wedding in her closet. These were the things of which forgotten afternoons of my childhood consisted. While Mom was outside gardening and Dad was at the office, and Palmer and Charles were at friends' houses, I explored the spaces previously closed off to me.

There had come a time, however, when I had learned that not all secrets were fun. At some point, I had discovered that my letters to the tooth fairy had been hidden underneath Mom's sweaters, that Santa Claus' handwriting matched that of my father. I never stopped wanting to know, though. I kept digging, kept rifling through things, even as my anticipation vacillated between excitement and dread. Looking into the abyss for answers, there's always a chance that, in addition to some glowing orb of uplifting light, there will be a fireball rocketing toward you, screaming that all your worst fears have been confirmed. My insatiable curiosity about the unknown was determined to outweigh my fear that one of my darker parallel lives would burst, flowing ceaselessly until it drowned my best intentions. From each mysterious chunk of text that I found in Gran's library, I would grasp for some grain of truth relevant to my reality. Over the course of the week leading up to Harvest Festival, between quizzing Kaye about her drug-addled youth and making elaborate flowcharts for the event, I found three more:

First,

"The world would have us believe that the expectation of love or happiness makes a person naive. That is not true. It is the expectation that a person has control over their own life that makes them naive. We're taught to amble amongst tall grass and wildflowers praising God for all the beauty given us, with no attention to the stones He has lodged in our paths that trip us. Adriel once seemed the very hole in the earth that God had sent me to fill. He was a man of the world who had traveled, surveyed, and found everything but his own soul. I stand next to this shell of a man, a decoration, now holding a baby boy like some sort of garnish. Behind the shell, though, the numbers and metals, this man is little more than a vulnerable fetus, unable to express emotion except through ragged cries, unable to digest food, unable to breathe without assistance. There was hope in the days when I believed that the sun would keep rising. Mostly now I know that the sun always sets, and rather than peaceful sleep, night means only a crying baby, another incarnation of the man who cannot feel. When love becomes a matter not only of thought rather than feeling, but a matter of confusion, it is no longer love. And now there exists a living, breathing reminder that I was made to believe in love by someone barely capable of it. Mother and Father always cling to propriety as though it were morality. Were I a stronger person, perhaps I would feel compelled to do the same. But my morality has been dashed upon rocks with life, marriage, and child. Propriety is nothing more than the shell a malformed person wears because they cannot live life without it. I have arms full of broken expectations, and lost control, and all I want is to be naive, to think the world a wonderful place. I cannot."

Well, I thought, whatever happened to enjoying youth? One of the other notes would surely be more illuminating.

"I used to think being beautiful meant being strong. That if I were unflappable, perhaps, and rosy-cheeked, life would be a game for me. But rose bushes aren't strong. Their branches are limp, their blossoms destroyed in a heavy rain. I feel as though the rest of my life will be one continuous thunderstorm, and my petals are already flopping to the ground to be trampled underfoot. I find I do not know what will happen to me, but even if I survive, I must write myself down, a psalm for my wishes, an ode to beauty, even as it is fragile and fickle. I could stay and speak words aloud, but there is some sense of serenity that is marred the moment my feelings leave my mouth. Once spoken, words are expelled into the world, they can mix in with grit and smog. They become, exhaled, the same thing that all other life is made of: dirt and dew. My story will stay hidden in books that Adriel will covet but never read. It will remain imbued with my heart, if only a little. And that is why, perhaps, I have felt compelled to write rather than to say. An imperfect memory of an imperfect life, but mine, all mine.

In the beginning, God created the earth. In my beginning, not even Plodis existed. Just a stout, dusty road that went past my father's saloon and on to the mill, through the forest. My father and mother loved God first, me and my little sister Klara second, and materials third. My childhood now seems an endless cycle of prayers and lessons and sneaking into the forest when Mama took her afternoon rests. When I was twelve or thirteen, that's when things began to hasten. Democracy was still young then, laws were soft and stretchy. And, selling industry as God's work, Adriel Weston came from the east. He built the factory and suddenly the dusty road was home to an endless stream of laborers, and it wasn't a break in the forest anymore. It was the city of Plodis and the trees around it were being cut down. He built a great marble house up the river and invited the family to a party. Uncomfortable amongst all those people, and determined to escape the leers that I felt hit my skin like spitting grease in a hot frying pan, I stole out onto the terrace. But Adriel followed me and I turned around to escape once more, only to find tears streaming down his face, almost pooling in his hollow cheeks. He has never said he loved me, but I was sure then that I could detect it in his eyes, some happiness, as though I were a forgotten childhood treasure. I was a child: sixteen. But all I had ever wanted was for someone to make me smile rather than beg forgiveness for my sins. Now, outside, the icy river is just visible between the brittle skeletons of what little trees remain, and I realize that the only dubious evidence of Adriel's love for me, not the idea of me, but me is bound in a single moment, an encounter six years ago on that damned terrace. All I have anymore is the allusion to love for someone that I never was to begin with."

I was confused now, but I kept reading, still hopeful for a positive turn, rather than more autobiography.

"We were married not long after the party, and I moved from the rooms above the simple clapboard saloon and across the river to this cold, white mausoleum filled with chairs nobody but me has sat in, books nobody but me has read. And there's a baby, and everyone thinks him precious and beautiful, and I cannot. I suppose I ought to be grateful that instead of slaving away in a kitchen for a drunkard and children, I can sit in electric light and numbly listen to a victrola while someone else cooks and someone else nurses my child. The dreams I used to have at night have invaded my days now, and I sit on the rocks with a torn dress and wild hair and think that my dreams must live, in their solitude and beauty, right in the middle of the river, or in the lake. Away from a place where I can tell the difference between night and day, between the safety of the shore and the silence of the deep, my heart dies a little each day."

I had figured out from the family tree that H probably referred to Hestia, which was the name of Pop's mother's sister. But then there was all this writing about her being married to Adriel, which was Pop's father's name, and this confused me. The words in these letters, writings, whatever they could be called, came in and out of my head and they didn't necessarily make sense, but they clung to me, like a magnet to an anvil. I couldn't understand them but something in them understood me. I had kept searching, maybe, because there was some part of me in these letters, a permission in them that I wanted to give myself. But then, I thought, I had anti-depressants and birth control and free will. I had nowhere near the obstacles that this woman professed to have. The person who had written these was holding out a hand, and as comforting as that might have seemed on the surface, I found some small freedom in the ability to reject it. Tyler was already holding my hand.

Harvest Festival came, and Tyler and I went because we were expected to go. Large, bright utility lights had been brought in, making the park look like some sort of poor man's baseball diamond. They hurt my eyes and caused me to squint, and I felt disoriented, and I could feel the stares. I imagined the thoughts running through people's heads. That attractive, young, smart boy with that girl who couldn't put down the cookies? What could she possibly be thinking would happen? Why would she expect anything at all?

"Addie," Katherine Holt called out, "Who's this handsome fella on your arm?"

Of course she already knew who Tyler was, and they began making compulsory small talk, while I went to get us glasses of apple cider. I knew what she was thinking: that Tyler was just being charitable spending time with me, that he was either going to wind up marrying a more attractive girl or be gay. Her eyes, full of reverence and concern, made that perfectly clear. It was October, but there was still warm, sticky humidity in the air, and a visible layer of shiny oil on everyone's faces. Everyone except Nan, who was holding Leo, and talking to another mom while the other kids chased each other across the grass. Wagon rides through the forest provided a regular audio loop of "Boos" followed by a chorus of children screaming. I had the feeling that I was stuck in petroleum jelly, unable to move at a regular pace, while more able-bodied gnats buzz buzz buzzed around me. Tyler's hand on the small of my back every so often reminded me that I was of the world, even if I wasn't in it. I wanted to be in it. But that wasn't going to happen while gap-toothed children struggled through caramel apples and flabby-armed grandmas talked about who'd had work done. I wanted, more than anything, to return to the snug nest I had imagined for the two of us in the garagepartment, away from prying eyes, away from the places where I felt paralyzed and slow—behind the curve. As we walked out of this backward ode to wholesome family ties, my eyes met Eduardo's. Of all the people there, I had the least to prove to him, and after a couple of seconds he looked away. All these feelings of isolation among so many people made me feel very much like crying, but when Tyler asked if I was okay, I nodded and smiled.

Though Lennie texted me ideas for couples' Halloween costumes almost every night, I couldn't bring myself to become excited about this prospect. Besides, costumes in Ravine were for people who had kids. Comfortably isolated from parenthood, I knew what it really meant, this dressing up and trawling for candy like an overloaded shrimping boat. It was another cry of complacency, "Look at us! We're full now. Someone carved a jack-o'-lantern shaped hole in each of us when we were young, but each time a baby is born, or a cute picture is taken, or a piece of candy is dropped in an orange plastic bucket, the hole becomes a little smaller." Even as they said it, their empty eyes betrayed that they didn't believe it. They were ashamed that they didn't believe it, and so they began to proclaim their happiness louder and all the time, not understanding why they didn't feel the way they said. But I knew. There was a leak in that space they kept on filling. Each time they said they were happy, a bit of happiness dribbled out, like blood from a wound. And no fun-size Milky Way bar or handful of Tootsie Rolls was going to fix that. But Beggars' Night continued, year after year, children going door to door, trying to patch up a wound that hadn't been theirs in the first place, and I sat next to my mother while she passed out candy, telling myself to stop being so damn cynical.

Eduardo sat in the background, discreetly recording pedestrian sounds just as he had on the Fourth of July. I told little kids that I liked their costumes and smiled at parents who asked me what I was up to. Nan and Palmer and the nephews and nieces had already been by—adorable as usual—and I found myself successively losing interest as my mother insisted on rehashing each interaction with people I didn't know.

"Dorothy from *The Wizard of Oz*," she would say, "I mean, do kids even watch that anymore?" or

"I just don't know what Brenda's going to do when Lucy goes to kindergarten next year."

I wanted, on some level, to be able to fulfill my daughterly duties, whatever that meant. But I felt my happy face slipping away with each stupid comment, and knowing that I couldn't become surly with the neighbors, I went inside. I needed to go somewhere less frenzied, less dependent on my ability to be consistently cheerful. I grabbed my bag and set out for the conservatory, not because the plants needed care, but because I did. I crept out of the driveway in my car, mindful of not crashing into any young ghouls or goblins.

There was something comforting about the drive through Plodis to the University, through streets that had long been forgotten by Ravinites because they didn't lead anywhere profitable. There were whole neighborhoods that may have been sparsely populated with people, and were, in that sense, alive, but were somehow magical because I knew that nobody in these pockets of shutters with slats missing and rusty barbed-wire fences gave a flying fuck about what I was doing with my life. Abandoned buildings and dusty old corridors had no stake in whether I was making use of my degree or in whether I was doing all that I needed to be doing to be married and popping out kids within a couple of years. I could be dead and decomposing in a vacant lot somewhere and these places and the people in them would keep on going as if nothing had happened. There was freedom in that, in the feeling that weeds could grow through me and the whole world wouldn't fall apart. Outside Ravine, I had the freedom to decay as much as I had the freedom to love someone, to marry someone, to hate someone.

I walked into the brick building as I had so many times before, through the glass and metal doors that were permanently dusty, and down that hallway, itself a testament to things easily forgotten. I don't know why I thought some grand and unusual lesson was going to leap out at me from the textured glass or peeling lettering on the doors. "Storage," "Staff Only," "Private." I stopped for a moment to hear myself think, but then I heard something else. Heavy breathing, muffled moans. I froze, not really because of the nature of the sounds themselves, but because what I saw was completely counter to what I heard. Maybe it was my fault that I hadn't automatically thought, "Wow! I bet that storeroom would be a great place for a tryst."

The two parties, for I assumed there were only two, climaxed simultaneously, which I was sure was fake. In my stunned state, I hadn't considered that there would be no cause for post-coital pillow talk. There weren't, after all, any pillows. There were old microscopes and trays of chipped glass slides and jarred biological specimens. I heard footsteps and ducked into one of the adjacent rooms, keeping the door open a crack to see who had been faking orgasms next to textbooks that smelled like formaldehyde. I was a bit taken aback to see George's mousey research assistant. Her frizzy, tight brown curls, normally tamed in an unforgiving bun, were hanging down upon her shoulders in odd clumps, her normally wan complexion replaced by two cheek-sized stains of berry color, the perspiration on her upper lip visible, and her bony arms more lively looking than I had ever seen them. I couldn't quite believe it, but Lennie had told me throughout college when I was wallowing in singleness, "The freaks always find someone." A couple seconds later my heart nearly stopped, when George came out after her, looking no more or less disheveled than usual.

I had expected another young, pimply-faced student, someone who would have chosen this mediocre specimen of woman over my aunt, the ex-model. I knew that Kaye found security and identity in being with this man who seemed stoic and safe and too interested in the science of life to partake directly in the dangerous business of being alive. What would she do if she found out he was more sand than rock? George and conquest both walked toward the conservatory, toward the hermetically sealed doors that locked in perfectly measurable units of life. I felt trapped again, trapped, trapped, trapped behind an open door, and though I have always sincerely hated the act of running, it seemed appropriate. Not toward the sanctuary that I had sought, but back into the claws of the one I had tried to leave behind. Obviously, I couldn't call anyone in my family. Lennie wasn't good at keeping secrets. So, in the driver's seat of my used car, I listened to the rings on Tyler's phone before he finally picked up.

"Hey," he said, "Where are you?"

"Well, I was going to the conservatory," I said.

"On Beggars' Night?" he said. I steamrolled past his question.

"But when I got here, I heard people fucking and so I hid in this room and then George and his research assistant came out of this other room and I left and I don't know what to do."

"Did he see you?" he asked.

"No," I said, feeling acutely the lumps that had begun to rise in my throat.

"Well you're golden, then."

"That's not the issue," I said, "The issue is that I just caught my uncle cheating on my aunt."

"How long have they been married?"

"I don't know," I said, "Like twenty years."

"Well, I guess it's not that surprising, then."

"I guess." I said. I knew that logically—statistically—he was right. Half of all marriages end in divorce and some crazy percentage of partners are unfaithful at one time or another. But no matter how much logic you apply to a situation, nothing can really and truly expunge feelings completely. Those bastards are always there, waiting to force themselves onto your instability once again. There had been very few times in my life when I couldn't push down hurt, anger, anything raw or real back down inside, when I couldn't act like everything was fine even when it wasn't. And when those moments came, it was like Robert Frost was there presenting me with two roads diverging in a fucking yellow wood. But the paths, both the normal one and the less traveled one, had become overgrown, so that the only thing I could do was freeze and wait for relief. I froze that night, too. I hung up the phone and threw it into the back of the car, and drove myself home, glassy-eyed and conscious only of the next step necessary for my survival. When I had been very drunk in college, and my concept of spatial and sensual reality melted like ice cream around my ankles, I had instructed myself, moment by moment, on how to keep from drowning.

Walk now. Walk straight. Cross the street now. Outpace the creepy man walking in the same direction. Get out your key. Look at the lock. Put the key in the lock. Look closely. Try again. Stop fumbling. Control your hands. Open the door. Go to the bathroom. Stick a finger down your throat. Lay down on your side. Not on your back. Your side. Don't die. Stay alive.

I got back to the house and pulled in the driveway. My mother had closed the front door and turned out the porch light—an unsubtle sign that Beggars' Night was over, and if you dared to ring the doorbell and ask for some candy, you'd be met with a glare from a stern middle-ager who was done with your bullshit. There was a light on in the pool house.

Open the car door. Walk now. Walk straight. Knock on the door.

Eduardo opened it quickly. I didn't know what to say, so I walked past him, into the pool house, eyes fixed on the wall.

"Addie?" he said.

He took my arm and turned me around, where I imagine he could see the tears pooling in my eyes, and making wet tracks down my cheeks. He asked what was wrong. I didn't answer because I couldn't. He hugged me and I felt my body buckle beneath me, my usually straight spine curling in spite of itself. I closed my eyes, willing myself to rise above my fragility. I opened them and pulled away.

"I found George cheating on Kaye," I said.

"What, here?" he said. I shook my head.

172

"At the conservatory."

"I'm sorry," he said. I moved my mouth to speak, but no sound came out. I tried again.

"I just don't understand," I said, sitting in the awful recliner on top of the awful carpet.

"It's this town," Eduardo said, "Everybody who chooses to live here is already dead. They're resigned to a living death."

"This is my home," I choked.

"Your uncle wouldn't be cheating if he already felt alive, that's all."

"Jesus," I said, "Can you just stop philosophizing for two seconds and tell me everything is going to be okay?"

"Maybe that's not what you need to hear," he said, "Maybe the whole meaning of this is for you to realize that things are not always alright."

"Are you serious?" I said, "How can you, of all people, not understand why this is upsetting for me?" I got up to go.

"Life is cruel, Addie," he called after me as the shitty screen door slammed shut behind me and I shivered in the cold of the patio. He called my name once or twice, trying to atone by luring me back inside, but I couldn't move. A minute or so later, I was blinded by headlights turning into the driveway. Jesus, I thought, perfect, another person to explain my fucking tears to. The lights flicked off and Tyler emerged from the driver's side. His face looked something like remorse, and I walked over.

"Are you okay?" he said, brushing his fingertips across my cheek. I shook my head, but the moment for tears had come and gone, so all he had to look at was the inky aftermath present in my irises, dead and unfeeling. He took my face in both of his hands and pulled me closer.

"I'm sorry," he said. "Listen. Everything's going to be okay." I opened my mouth, fully prepared to vomit out some vulnerable blather, clutching his wrists as they held up my face like epithelial buttresses or something. But my vulnerability had already been macerated and swallowed and I couldn't bring it to life again, so I kissed him instead.

"Come on," he said, "Come over."

I nodded and walked to the passenger side of the car. Eduardo had closed the pool house door.

NOVEMBER

I n school, at some point, I had learned about people flock-
ing to Shirley Temple movies during the Depression for an
escape from life. Even before that, I always wanted my life to be
similarly cinematic. I've wanted for the tragedies around me to
get lost in bright lights and orchestral music such that even the un-
fortunate bits of me would dazzle critics and blind audiences with
their beauty. Something terrible could be happening, but onlookers
would only be able to say, "Wow! I'm better for having seen that."
When you don't have a cinema to play film of your life, when you
don't have someone being paid millions to stage your life, you
have to rely on memories. I remember better with my eyes closed.
With my eyes closed, I hear dry leaves crunching underfoot, and
remember taking walks that November with Tyler. Eyes closed,
I smell fabric softener and remember cuddling with Leo on the
couch. On the dark fall-to-winter days, I would sit with my arm
around his tiny body. Even then, in that present, my thoughts alter-
nated between convincing myself that Leo would be fine in Ravine

and wistfully dreaming of Tyler whisking me away. I told myself maybe life turns out exactly how it is supposed to and tried not to entertain any other possibility. Almost every evening was spent at the garagepartment. They certainly weren't going to be spent at my parent's house, slinking up the carpeted stairs to be met by my mother's disapproving looks and snide comments about the "new styles" of underwear I had bought. Without sounding like a simpering twat, I had come to the realization that my mother had, at least during my lifetime, been fairly unpredictable next to my father, whose predictability was thorough and unflagging. This mixture made for a caustic, festering chaos. The garagepartment, and all it represented, was the base to the acid of my filial home.

I told myself that Tyler was perfect, and against all that I had been trained to expect, he certainly seemed that way. I thought about the picture-perfect moments when we watched fireworks from his rich-kid treehouse, or he came to rescue me in his nice car. Were those what I had wished for when I wanted my life to play beautifully for others? Why couldn't I let my life be beautiful for myself? But Tyler and I were more than a series of pretty images.

"How was Leo today?" he asked one day.

"Sweet," I'd said, "he reminds me a lot of myself."

"Oh? How's that?"

"He's weird. I don't know, I just went through so much cliquey bullshit in elementary school and the thought of him having to do the same just breaks my heart a little."

Tyler's eyes automatically fixated on a spot on the wall just so that the rest of his being could engage with me.

"Well," he said, "You turned out okay."

"Yeah."

"You can't feel everybody else's feelings for them, you know," he said, "You've just got to grow a thicker skin...I had to."

"Yeah," I said.

I brushed it off at the time, telling myself he was probably right. I was reading too much into things. I needed to focus on the happy things in my life. They did look amazing, my happy moments, as if a team of highly paid people had spent months planning them, but for all their beauty, and their soundtracks, and their perfect lighting, even when I was in them, I was still a spectator. When you're overstimulated by the visual, you can only speculate as to what should be felt, not what is actually felt. At the time, I mostly didn't like feelings, not yet having figured out that they were the only thing keeping me alive. I was, per Tyler's suggestion, working on growing a thicker skin, but in the end, what did that actually mean? The very phrase implied that one's epidermis was constantly under some sort of attack. And if this were the case, telling someone to grow a thicker skin seemed a decidedly Republican thing to say. In the same vein as, "Oh, you're poor? Pay more taxes. It'll totally help." Why was the focus on the perfectly normal depth of the skin and not at the assholes who were firing darts or something at it?

And so, I got myself into another philosophical inner dialogue about nothing, and thought I sounded like Eduardo, whom I'd successfully avoided since Beggars' Night. Maybe I should have grown a thicker skin, and maybe I shouldn't have thought so much about how the wrongs of my childhood might be revisited on my kin, but at the end of the day, the sun was still setting and when it's dark out, hypotheticals don't matter, do they? What mattered was that there was enough artificial light to live in with no limit or regard for what was natural.

Mom had originally talked about having a going-away reception for Eduardo at some repurposed warehouse in Plodis, but Gran, upon hearing of this plan, swiftly did some repurposing of her own. She, of course, loathed Eduardo, and everything disrespectful and pedestrian he stood for. But the combination of his persona and some "trendy" venue with exposed brick and "original industrial features" seemed to offend Gran to her very core. Of course, Gran told mother, the reception would have to be held at the house. I secretly thought that was exactly what mother wanted all along. Now Gran would take care of everything and Mom wouldn't have to lift a finger. Of course Tyler and his parents would be invited, and I was determined that this not be a repeat of the Harvest Festival. I couldn't get lost in my thoughts. I had to flaunt my improved social status to all of the PTA mothers who had thought me a strange child in elementary school. I wasn't sure exactly what I meant for this to accomplish or why I felt that I had anything at all to prove.

Nonetheless, my unspoken insistence that I could, indeed, mix into society with the best of them had me in a new dress—a red one, a crepey, flowing thing that I could wear lacy tights and Mary Janes under. My hair pulled back, my makeup done, and my eyes unable to shake the starstruck, fuck-me expression that is, for better or worse, my default, I felt quite powerful. There was some unobtrusive jazz in the background, and Katherine's inescapable voice could be heard prattling on from the other side of the ballroom. My heart skipped a beat when I saw Tyler in a suit. I wanted him to march right over and rescue me from whatever stale conversation I was engaged in. That didn't happen, and now I'd fallen behind and could no longer smile and nod with the same conviction. As Tyler piled a plate high with crudités, I sidled over to him.

"Hey, stranger," I said, imagining myself, in the red dress, to be sultry and irresistible, like a Midwestern Lauren Bacall.

"Hey," he said.

I was intent on being perfect, on not disappointing myself, and so I pretended not to notice that he seemed nervous and withdrawn, except for when he had to light up and talk to people. At some point during the long barrage of toasts being made to Eduardo, Tyler motioned to me that he was going outside, and of course, I followed. I always followed. As we walked out the front door and down the drive, I shivered in the cold, and he took off his jacket and gave it to me. I wondered if it could get any more Old Hollywood? Could this collection of moments be any more antiquated and charming? I hoped that Katherine Holt had seen us leave and that she and my mother would discuss my success over skinny lattes. We walked onto the sidewalk, underneath the trees and obnoxiously bright streetlights. I could hardly contain my happiness. This is what love is, I thought, this feeling that walking in heels on a dirty sidewalk in the middle of winter will never be topped by anything grander. Across the street, an older couple walked past, holding hands with a small, fluffy dog a couple of steps ahead of them.

"You know, I have trouble believing in marriage, given my parents," Tyler said, "But you look at people like that and you just know they're better off for being together."

All I could do was murmur an affirmative reply. Finally, finally, these wonderful romanticisms that I never fully believed in were showing themselves not only to be true, but to be true for me, true in my life. So he hadn't said "I love you." He'd given me his jacket, and he was waxing philosophical on the merits of spending one's entire life with another. That was all I needed.

Eduardo left the next morning. I heard him piling his shit into the station wagon to be driven to the airport and I heard my mother loudly contemplating whether she ought to wake me so that I could say goodbye. Eduardo said no, that we'd said our goodbyes the night before, which was a lie. The car doors closed and it was silent again. I knew that a couple of hours later, the parents would be back and I would want to be gone. I wasn't quite sad that Eduardo was leaving. He condemned things—my life, my community—without really knowing what he was talking about. He'd made me feel confused.

I needed somewhere hermetic and quiet. A place so quiet that no one else's thoughts suffocated me, pressing down against me in a space that could only hold a certain amount of humanity. I had thought, for at least a little while, that the conservatory could be that space, but that certainly wasn't the case anymore. Even an aseptic space that was supposed to be purely academic had been sullied by feelings. I turned the latest pages of writing over and over in my fingers as I sat in a chunky oversize sweater on the patio, trying to reconcile the rare autumn sun with the crispness of the breeze. Drunk on the promise of self-realization, I walked lazily over to Gran and Pop's, bypassing the house entirely and continuing through the woods toward the river.

Try as I might, I couldn't banish constant thought from my mind. If I rubbed the toe of my boot through the brush and pine needles until it hit hardened earth, or brushed my fingers across the moss on a tree trunk, I felt and didn't think so much. I imagined a beating heart within each tree, covered in moss, soft, unhardened, and pulsing. I felt my own heart beating in time, wishing for Tyler and I to occupy a defined place in the world, where I could survive on heartbeats alone, and never think again, and where whatever happened to me was due to a fate I had no control over. I wanted to be a tree, conscious only of the fact that there was dirt below me and sky above me, that I was either alive or dead. A tree doesn't have questions or thoughts. It doesn't care if it's going to die because of the Emerald Ash Borer or because of a burly man named Gunther wielding an axe.

The forest, the cold, the idea of a thoughtless existence, calmed me. The blood running through my veins was just sap. Still, I would not be able to replace my brain with a bunch of wooden rings until I had figured out who had written the papers I'd found in the library. Once I had solved this mystery, I felt I would be able to either move on or become comfortable with remaining the same. Then, maybe, I'd be able to slip into the cozy nap of adulthood. Who didn't love a good nap? It was comfortable, soothing, just the thing a lost and lonely child needed. My head laid against a scratchy tree trunk for the split second before I remembered that bugs lived on trees, I contemplated looking in the drawer with the family tree again. I knew I wouldn't find any new information there, so I set out in another direction. I walked to the square, then down one of the side streets to a tiny cottage-like house that had somehow survived years of "improvement" and now housed the Ravine Historical Society.

A white-haired woman seated at a desk inside looked up, evidently quite surprised to see me—another person, and a young one at that—in front of her.

"Can I help you, dear?" she asked.

"Yes. I'm looking for information on the Weston family."

"Yes, okay. Have a seat and I'll find the file."

I sat, feeling a little as though I must be disturbing something. Does history hate very much to be disturbed, I wondered? Does it lounge in damp spaces, strategizing over what it will do if suddenly caught in the beam of a flashlight? She came back holding a binder that had cleverly been disguised as a shabby-chic canvas box.

"Now, most of this relates to the factory," she said, and I nodded, acting as though I had the faintest clue as to what she was talking about. As she resumed her post at the desk, I began to flip through the plastic encased documents therein.

"Oh," she said, "If you want to handle any of the documents

directly, we do have gloves."

I nodded and smiled. There were old invoices for Weston Inc. I suppose I should have known exactly what the family produced, but all I had ever been told was that Pop's father had been in the steel business before he went into finance.

"I'm sorry," I said, "Do you know what this g.v. stands for?"

"Oh, uh-huh," she said, "Grave vault. That's what the factory made, you know."

"What's a grave vault?"

"Well, it seems that around the turn of the century, there was a lot of real concern about grave robbers and so this Adriel Weston began manufacturing these coffins that were impossible to break into. He seems to have been quite successful up until the fire."

"Fire?"

"Yes," she said, "in the 1920s I believe." She came back and flipped through more pages in the file, until she reached a newspaper print of a huge blaze.

"Yeah," she said, "The whole place caught fire and was completely destroyed, and I'm not sure they ever rebuilt. The owner seems to have gotten into banking after. His descendants still live in Ravine, though."

"Thanks," I said, and she proceeded to sit back at her desk, gumming a peppermint quite loudly. There appeared to be an unmistakable penchant for omitting the truth in my family. Aunt Kaye's apparent involvement with drugs, these writings and their suggestion that the good old days hadn't been so good, the devastating fire that no one had ever thought to mention.

"This is all you have?" I asked.

"Mm-hmm. But you know Ravine Library has microfilms of the Plodis newspaper from the time of its inception, if you want to look there."

The next day, Leo strapped into the stroller, I set out for the library. He fell asleep on the walk there, and I rocked the stroller with one foot while I scrolled through old newspapers in a dark corner of the reference section. I began with the date of the fire and found a front-page article.

"An employee of the Weston Vault Factory, Francis Haberkern, having grown increasingly upset at the poor wages and long hours at Weston appears to have deliberately organized and carried out an incendiary attack on the factory, located on Spruce Street in Plodis. Great black plumes of smoke could be seen above the factory Saturday night as the volunteer fire brigade and many Plodis residents tried to quench the flames. Nearly 400 men were employed by owner Adriel Weston in the construction of grave vaults. It appears that irreparable damage has been done to the structural integrity of the building, and Mr. Weston does not intend to rebuild."

None of this got me any closer to understanding the writings I had found in the library. All I felt now was confusion about whether I should feel protective of my great-grandfather, who had evidently been kind of a dick, but was good at making money, or whether I should feel ashamed that his self-interest had adversely impacted the lives of so many others. Leo began to stir a bit, and I resumed my rocking of the stroller, begging in my head for five more minutes to explore my history, sure that it held the key to my future.

A tiny column hidden in the pages of the newspaper from a couple days later caught my eye:

"Woman Found Dead in Oak Lake"

"Hestia Weston, wife of Weston Vault Company owner Adriel Weston, was found dead, apparently of drowning, in Oak Lake. It seems that Mrs. Weston had been missing ever since the 18th of May, the night of the Weston Factory fire. The death is believed to be a suicide, as several heavy stones were found in the pockets of Mrs. Weston's dressing gown. She is survived by her husband and infant son, Gareth, as well as her father, mother, and sister."

I felt frozen again, the logical path for thoughts in my head deteriorated. All of the subjects demanding my attention were chipping and clawing away at my ability to think. But Leo had really and truly woken up now and was staring at me through sleepy eyes. I switched off the microfilm.

"Want to go read some stories?" I asked.

I heard myself reading a 1950s children's book about Thanksgiving, but my mind was somewhere else. I kept wondering whether I could have read the family tree wrong. Was there some very simple explanation for my confusion? Surely there was something that explained why I felt as though I had never seen the name Hestia, something that explained why I had always thought Pop's mother's name was Klara. Why had this H.W., which I now assumed stood for Hestia Weston, been compelled to write these soul-baring notes that said everything and nothing at the same time? Why had she needed to hide them between the pages of books? How was it that they had never before been uncovered? What was the real story behind the fire? Was my role, almost one hundred years later, to expose some sort of truth, or to guard the family secrets? In the meantime, the real world was wriggling in my lap, unable to keep himself still for the last few pages. I picked up the pace. I wanted to finish the story.

"And they all held hands and sang songs and were grateful that they had each other."

At the beginning of November, Gran and Pop had traveled to Bermuda to visit one of Gran's friends from boarding school. In years past, they had made it a point to return before Thanksgiving, but this year proved different. Gran had called Nancy, of all people, to tell her that they planned to stay on the island for a while longer—which meant that they wouldn't be at the house to host the usual family gathering. It was strange, not within their usual sphere of behavior. But perhaps, as with the Harvest Festival, Gran was tired of carrying on tradition. She *was* eighty-four years old. So she had passed the reins to another hallowed tradition on to someone she knew would carry it off faultlessly. Nan took this assignment very seriously and planned an elaborate menu, assigning all of us dishes to contribute. While my mother had obviously become a disciple of post-Cold-War food, she couldn't bear to impose her new tastes upon family traditions. This holiday had begun before anyone knew what the hell chia seeds were—before anyone even knew that cigarettes were bad for you. They should continue that way. She railed against the idea that anyone would presume to tell her what to cook.

"She sent me a recipe for some garlicky medley of mashed cauliflower and parsnips and low-starch potatoes. What the hell is that? I'm not making that. I'll make my mother's mashed potatoes like I've always done, with a pound of butter. None of this 'gourmet' bullshit on Thanksgiving."

I had been given the task of making some sort of herbed rolls, an easy recipe, something she didn't think I could fuck up. I had no reason to rebel. Like my mother, Kaye had lamented her charge of making a pie with fresh pureed pumpkin, a brown-butter crust, and crème fraîche. Tyler would be spending the day with family in Cleveland, and so I resigned myself to a day with no escape from family, and a fight between Nan and Mom about proper Thanksgiving cookery, if I was lucky.

The day of, I appeared to be the only sous-chef who had actually followed my marching orders. My mother had filled a large crock with Idaho potatoes that contained lots of salt and an entire block of full-fat cream cheese. Kaye arrived late, and nearly threw a bakery box containing a pumpkin pie and a tub of Cool Whip onto Gran's kitchen counter. Nan pretended not to be pissed, but of course she was. She couldn't have viewed Kaye and Mom's refusal to follow directions as anything less than a big "fuck you" and an implicit reminder that the only person who could get away with Gran-like behavior was Gran. Nan had wanted a promotion within the family, but she was out of luck. Even without the requisite matriarch and patriarch, the roles played were exactly the same, and all the actors had been waiting—in plain sight—for their time in the spotlight. Without Pop, conversation fell to Palmer and Dad. My mother filled Gran's enforcer role effortlessly. I didn't mind not having a speaking role in this ensemble. I had never seen any of these archetypes—matriarch, eager young wife, black sheep—as spaces that I would fill at some point, when a regular player was absent and needed an understudy. Kaye and George were being oddly smiley and affectionate toward each other, and I wondered if she knew of his infidelity and was trying to put forth an image of married bliss for Darwin, or the rest of her family, or just herself.

"How's school going?" I asked Darwin.

"It's okay," he said, "Boring mostly. But we get to pick our own book to do a book report about before Christmas, so at least there's that."

"Yeah? Have you decided what book you're going to write about?"

"*No Exit* by Jean-Paul Sartre."

"Impressive."

"Not really," he said, "The language is fairly simple."

"So you've already read it then?"

"I'm almost done. Have you read it?"

I nodded.

"Well," I said, "What's your analysis?"

"Well the whole idea of the book is that Hell is other people, right? I'm going to argue the parallels between that and the Ravine School System."

I laughed, "Sounds about right. Thought I'm not sure your teacher will appreciate the reference."

"She won't," he said, "She gets flustered whenever I'm too smart for her, but she's stuck with me for another 122 days."

"Counting down are you?"

"Didn't you?"

"School will get better when you're older," I said.

He nodded, because he didn't know what else to do, and because we both wanted to believe that the statement I had just made was true. I drank wine and pretended to watch football and texted Tyler. We made plans to meet at the coffee shop for hot chocolate as soon as he got home a few days later.

I smiled when he walked into Starbucks, adorably disheveled and in a scarf. He was someone I didn't have to pretend with.

"Want to walk and talk?" he said.

"Sure. So, you survived your family, huh?"

"Barely."

"You want to talk about it?"

"Nah. How was yours?"

"Oh, fine. I talked to Darwin. He's going to write a book report comparing *No Exit* to the Ravine School System. Can you believe it? Sartre at nine," I laughed.

"That sounds like it will be a mess."

"I think it's sort of brilliant. Hell consisting of other people sounds like it pretty much sums up my experience. He's a smart kid."

"You know, I find it a bit incredible that you discussed Sartre with a nine-year-old."

"What about it do you find incredible? The fact that I would be having meaningful conversations or the fact that a nine-year-old might be?"

"Mostly the nine-year-old."

"Mostly?"

"Fine. All the nine-year-old. Though the fact that you get something out of it is pretty compelling evidence that you're not quite right."

"Hilarious, you fucker."

"Do you use that language when you're talking to Darwin?"

"Yeah, I do, actually," I said.

He smiled an odd smile; we turned onto his street, and I took his hand. He gripped back and I felt happiness and relief. Suddenly he pulled his hand free and punched at the air in front of the maple tree we were walking past.

"Thanksgiving must really have sucked, huh?" I said. He shook his head. I guess I should have been more alarmed at his behavior, but if anyone understands being unable to healthily express rage after spending time with family, it's me.

I rubbed his shoulders, "What's up?"

"I don't know," he said, "I just worry that...I don't know. Too much time with my family. It's hard for me to believe that I'll ever be anything but exactly like them."

"Hey. Don't talk like that. You're not your parents, and your life will be whatever you want it to be. Look at me. Everything will work out."

He looked at me, but it was like he didn't see me. He kissed me, we kept walking, and I felt happy again. Back in the garage-partment, I sat on the couch while he went to the bathroom. He came back and laid his head in my lap and I felt like I never wanted to leave. Anyone can be in love when they're happy. It's the being in love through hardship and sadness that makes it seem like it could last forever.

"There's some Hitchcock movie on TV soon," he said, "Do you want to watch it?"

"Um, what time is it?" He got up to check his phone.

"5:35."

"Shit, I should get going to Gran's for dinner."

"Twice in one week?"

"Oh, you know, one impressive meal wasn't enough for Nan." I smiled at him.

"Oh, well, hold on," he said, a wild look in his eyes.

He crossed the room and perched on a windowsill, facing me. Suddenly all the little tells I had been writing off as passing annoyances or trivial hiccups, his distant eyes, his weird non-smile smiles, his punching a tree, came flooding into my brain.

"Listen," he began, "You know I really like spending time with you. But this isn't going to work."

"You like spending time with me?" I asked, "Is that what all this has been to you?"

As I tried not to cry and to absorb what the hell he had just said, he sat next to me on the couch, taking my hand and gently grazing his thumb back and forth across my open palm, comforting me as though he wasn't the cause of my upset. He punched a throw pillow. His actions, his false machismo, seemed to suggest that he was unhappy with the situation that he was presently creating. He didn't stop creating it. He didn't say anything, either. In the moment, I reacted how I had been trained to. I told myself I should have expected disappointment, that this was more of an inevitability than an unexpected surprise. I even asked him if *he* was okay. Soon, whatever porous moments there had been for exchange between us had passed, and I got up from the couch and headed for the door. In my state of shock, we exchanged pleasantries and an obligatory but unfeeling hug before I exited. Once outside, the fresh air, what sunshine was left in the sky, flipped the switch inside me; the one that said "Wait! Your feelings are here." Each step down that flight of stairs increased my indignance, and by the time I reached the foot of the driveway, a pretty steady stream of "what the fuck" was running through my head. As I called Lennie and hid behind the stone driveway post, the tears came hard and fast.

"Hello?"

"He fucking ended it." There was a pause, as she undoubtedly tried to decipher what I was saying or why my voice sounded strange.

"Tyler! He told me he liked spending time with me, but it wasn't going to work."

"What?" she squawked.

"This has been a waste of my fucking time. How did I ever think this would work?"

"Wait, wait, wait. That was all he said?"

"Yes."

"So weird."

"He held my fucking hand while we were walking around today. He didn't even bring it up until I told him I had to leave for dinner at Gran and Pop's."

"I'd be so pissed."

"I have to go. I'm going to be late for dinner, and I need to fix my face before I see my mother."

"Call me later. It'll be okay."

"Yeah."

I hurriedly wiped my eyes and took some deep breaths, tucking my emotions back where they belonged, scrunched up and out of sight. The family was already at the house. Mom, upon seeing my face, asked me if I was alright and gave me a hug. I wanted to say no, to be comforted, caressed, whatever that situation would garner in a nurturing family. But she didn't want to comfort me, not really. She knew that I had buried my feelings. She'd taught me how. It wasn't within her rights to dredge them up. I ate my dinner, but I didn't taste it. I heard the usual conversation, but I didn't listen to it.

That night, I went home and lay on my bed, reading and re-reading Hestia's writing that I had taken from Gran and Pop's library and hidden in my sock drawer. I looked for clues in these words, things through which I could have seen the break-up coming. I felt both blindsided and stupid for feeling blindsided. I felt like maybe Hestia had made more sense than I had wanted her to. But, then and there, staring at the tiny H.W. in the corner of the last letter, I felt like maybe if I could figure out that mystery, I would find some sort of silver lining to the dull pain that I felt. I fell asleep with the overhead light on, watching a movie on my laptop. I was numb, and for the first time in a long time, I did not want to be.

I would have to venture outside of Ravine for the truth. There was a county records repository near the university, so I drove there the next day. It was located in a large, aluminum, warehouse, and the only worker there appeared to be a man whose very appearance was quiet, with a fuzzy and balding head, unobtrusive wire-rim glasses, and an incomparably soft-looking argyle vest.

"Excuse me. I'm looking for some records."

"Do you have names?" he half whispered.

I nodded, sliding him the post-it note I had prepared at home with the names Adriel Weston, Hestia Weston, Klara Weston, and

Gareth Weston on it. He typed timidly on the outdated desktop he had behind the reference counter.

"Mm," he muttered to himself, "Right this way."

He led me noiselessly to a giant card catalogue, adjusting his pant leg before kneeling to retrieve several cards from a low drawer.

"Are you familiar with how to work a microfiche reader?" he asked.

I nodded. It was odd, I thought, that the official records of one's life should look so small and generic. Soon, however, enlarged and illuminated, there were Adriel Weston's birth and death certificates. There was nothing surprising or special about them, so I moved on to the next thin plastic sheet of life.

Klara Kroenkel Weston

Born 1 November 1907 to Hans and Maria Kroenkel

Died 26 November 1980 of natural causes.

Hestia Kroenkel Weston

Born 8 October 1904 to Hans and Maria Kroenkel

Died 18 May 1926 of suicide by drowning.

Gareth Adriel Weston

Born 2 February 1926 to Hestia and Adriel Weston.

Then, marriage certificates for Adriel and Hestia and Adriel and Klara. I kept pulling the transparencies on and off of the viewing dock, making sure I was seeing things correctly, and jotting down notes on paper as I tried to connect the dots. So Hestia had been Pop's biological mother, and had died only 3 months after giving birth to him. And then, only a year later, Adriel and Klara had married. I felt flustered and short of breath, as though I had stumbled upon a secret nobody ever wanted to know about, a secret exponentially more monumental than the fact that my mother was the tooth fairy. The quiet clerk smiled at me as I returned the microfiche to him. I couldn't smile back, and I got in my car and drove to Gran and Pop's with a sort of primal urgency. I wanted a solution to present itself, but it seemed the deeper I dug, the more confusing things became. I was in way too deep to stop now. I tried to remember the inspiration I had initially felt at finding Hestia's words, how I had interpreted them as symbols that Ravine had a place for me. But how could I take comfort in the words of someone who had not only *not* found a place here, but had decided that death was better than a lifetime lived in Ravine?

I raced into the house, the library, unsure of exactly what I was looking for. I stopped and closed my eyes, resting my hand on the waxy wooden desk, wishing for some trace of hope to leap out at me, some trace of a person who hadn't given up on life. There had to be something I had missed, I thought. There had to be a better answer, an answer that made life seem like less of an unwinnable game. I opened my eyes and turned around. The shelves were still there, in their brilliance, but I knew that I had searched each and every volume for hidden wisdom. This was the only room where books were kept in the entire house, at least any of the books old enough to have been there at the same time as Hestia. I turned back around and looked at the uncomfortable velvet loveseat, wondering whether or not Hestia had felt its springs digging into her back before she had decided to walk into deep waters. And there it was, between the horrid velvet settee, and the tapestried wingback chair, the only book I hadn't searched, on its polished wooden stand, the huge leather-bound family Bible, opened at the center.

I shut it and opened the front cover again, methodically turning each page. There was a section for recording births, baptisms, deaths, and marriages, but these pages were empty, save one entry. Under "Births" was written "Hestia Kroenkel Weston. 18 May 1926." It was *her* handwriting. I fished my notes from my purse. The date was the same as the night the warehouse had burned down. There was a Bible verse written there as well. Isaiah 9: 18-20. I turned to that page, and saw a thin paper, just like all of the others, only this one had been sealed with wax. I read the verses:

"For wickedness burneth as the fire; it devoureth the briers and thorns; yea, it kindleth in the thickets of the forest, and they roll upward in a column of smoke. Through the wrath of Jehovah of hosts is the land burnt up; and the people are as the fuel of fire: No man spareth his brother. And one shall snatch on the right hand, and be hungry; and he shall eat on the left hand and they shall not be satisfied: they shall eat every man the flesh of his own arm."

The passage intrigued me, but I wasn't ready for the story to be over yet. So I went home, and put the letter in my sock drawer like all the rest, wax still sealing what I knew to be the last undiscovered bit of her.

DECEMBER

Being sad about Tyler was objectively useless, and so I tried not to be. But there were practical considerations that were impacting me and that I couldn't completely suppress. There was, suddenly, no more sex, no more kisses, no more falling asleep next to someone, no more staring into eyes, no more laughter for two. I told myself that Tyler had been a jerk to me and that I was better off without him and what's more we had never been officially dating, so could I really even justify grieving? But my dreams didn't follow logic, and my mind wandered every so often to the walk-up with hanging plants we might eventually have lived in, to him telling me I was beautiful even if I had flour all over my face from baking pies.

Those falsehoods were much more sad post-relationship, even if they had been bullshit to begin with. I fell back into my post-collegiate funk. By the time a week had passed, my life once again revolved around sleeping, taking care of Leo, watching television, and sleeping some more. Such behavior wasn't unusual for that time of the year, with its gray skies and freezing temperatures. But the meteorology only makes it that much worse when you feel lousy about things that are completely unrelated to the weather.

I hadn't ever actually told my family that I was no longer seeing Tyler, but they seemed to have figured it out, if only because I was sleeping at home again. We didn't speak about it, of course. My father would give me a couple of extra pats on the head as he walked by the couch. My mother didn't hide the wine. They didn't talk about jobs even when all I did was lie on my bed or lie on the couch and stare at something: the TV, the wall, my split ends. There had been so many times I had wanted to keep from thinking over the past couple of months and here I was, finally in a fog of nothingness again. It wasn't sweet, though, or not as sweet as I had thought it would be, because the thoughts hadn't just floated away, had they? They were silenced, but whatever malaise had caused them in the first place remained.

It was an early morning in December, so early that the sun hadn't come up yet, and the night seemed endless and unforgiving. I opened my blinds, and surveyed the endless dark. That morning, when my puffy eyes detected thin snowflakes falling in and out of the misleading glow of the streetlight, I knew it was time. And so, in my baggy pajamas, the obfuscating dark of winter cloaking me, I went to my dresser, took out the folded paper and gently broke the wax seal.

"The factory is on fire. It is night and I can see the blaze from where I sit. For all their efforts to control life, they have brought about the apocalypse. They'll say I was crazy. I am not. Their sustenance is gotten through making life tolerable and dry, easy to digest. I do not want to be easy to digest. The heart is not to be macerated just because it is a tough piece of meat. Life is not something that you suffer through and swallow because it would be impolite not to. That is what I risk becoming if I stay here, some desiccated piece of meat that lacks flavor, that nourishes without pleasure. Perhaps, before long, my life will be forgotten, and written off as a freak occurrence among the normal passing of things. What they do not realize, and what I do realize, is that the world will always be defined by its outcasts, by the unintended ink stains on the page, by those we deem unwell or broken. The world I inhabit at the moment is one in which a stain means we must discard all it is that we have done and begin again. This world is one where the afflicted are locked away from the sun, hidden until they die and trees are cut down to build their coffins. Even new life begins under this shroud of death, for there is no way of knowing whether it is the kind of life that will be embraced as normal and allowed to breathe, or the type that is slowly killed in every way but that which is physical. I reject this pantomime of life, and in my death from it, I choose life as it is really meant to be: an endless summer beneath tree branches whose leaves absorb bitterness and give off love."

I already knew the ending, from the death certificate, of course, but the words that went with it struck me at my core. I had to leave my house, this structure that had been built so literally on the spoils of a man who had, directly or indirectly, caused the death of someone who wanted to be remembered even as she knew she'd be forgotten. I put on a coat, a scarf, and boots, and crept in the dark to the woods behind Gran and Pop's. I imagined the path Hestia must have walked to her death and felt sad and angry that she had been forced into a life that hadn't loved her back. I sat on a flat rock on the edge of the river and dipped my fingers in the freezing water long enough that I couldn't feel them anymore. Devoid of both feeling and thought—I imagined that's how she must have been, rocks in her pockets, deeper into the water with each step. I closed my eyes and added a new dream world to my head, one where I walked into water and escaped life.

The very edge of the faint morning sun was beginning to show, and I heard someone tromping through the woods. Though the chances of said person being a rapist or axe murderer was relatively small, I became anxious for a moment. I hadn't brought my phone and the steps did sound as though they were coming my way.

"Addie? What are you doing here?"

Fuck me. It was Tyler.

"Just taking a walk, yourself?"

"Oh, sometimes I go for morning runs in the woods."

"You go for morning runs in flannel and duck boots?"

He looked down and laughed weakly.

"Look," he said, "I'm sorry."

"Whatever," I said, getting to my feet to make my escape.

"You know why, though. You know why I had to end it."

"No, actually I don't know why. Perhaps you could enlighten me."

"This is never going to work, not really. You know that. You and me in Ravine. It doesn't make sense."

"How does it not make sense?"

"Our life would be made of constantly explaining ourselves to these assholes. We'd spend every day trying to convince every-one that our happiness is worth more than their conventions."

"Are you saying it's because I'm fat?"

"Not really."

"Not really? You are un-fucking-believable, you know that?"

"You don't honestly think we would work?"

"That's beside the point. The point is that your reasoning for why it wouldn't work is fundamentally flawed."

He sighed. I continued,

"Which means that you're actually just scared that it won't work, which means you think there's some universe where it could work, which means," my voice cracked, "you're a fucking coward."

"Maybe."

"What did you think was going to happen when you asked me to that movie? When I slept every night in your bed? What did you envision the endgame being?"

"I don't know."

"You told me I was beautiful. You told me you felt a warmth for me."

"I wasn't lying," he said.

"No. You weren't lying," I said, "You were just omitting the truth."

"Addie…" he touched my shoulder.

"No," I said, pulling away as he became a watercolor through my tears, "It makes perfect sense, actually. You're just as much of an asshole as I always thought you were and I'm just the quiet, bitter girl who makes herself unloveable."

I ran away before he could respond. There was enough time when I got home to sleep for a couple of hours before I had to go over and care for Leo, but I didn't sleep—and, after a while—I didn't even cry. Anything beyond lying limp and mute on my bed seemed like a gross burden. But life always went on, whether or not I moved forward with it. And so I put on my Ravine uniform: pink button-down, cardigan, jeans, driving mocs; like something out of a Lands End catalogue, and went to work.

I had always romanticized someday looking like a scorned woman in a bad romantic comedy—wearing sweatpants, bags under my eyes, hair in some sort of grease ball bun on my head, clutching tissues and half-melted ice cream, and somehow eliciting love and sympathy from the world around me because I had been abandoned. That would have been nice, but the truth was that it wasn't my style. I would have gotten some sort of pitying or judgmental look from my mother for my appearance, I always had bags under my eyes, and if I got my hands on ice cream, it was gone before it got all melty and sad. There was an assumption that my emotions would register in the way that I looked, that because

I wasn't overtly like a sad, vulnerable puppy, I didn't require comfort from others. But I looked the same on the outside whether I was sad, happy, or heartbroken. And maybe that's why Leo cooed at me and climbed on me and laughed as gleefully as always when knocking down block towers. I even felt guilty when I couldn't smile back at him very convincingly. It wasn't fair that he should have to feel anything that I was feeling. He hadn't made the decisions that had led me to my current predicament. He hadn't become dependent on someone else even though he knew better.

Because I couldn't love myself, I tried constantly to communicate to Leo that he deserved love—all of it—without condition, every moment of every day, not after he had made a goal in pee-wee soccer or when he had aced the SATs, but just exactly as he was. I was already broken. Maybe there was still hope for him. Anyway, his presence on my lap was comforting. I heard the back door open and looked at Leo expectantly, as I always did at that moment.

"Mommy's home," I said.

I was surprised to see Palmer in the kitchen.

"Oh…hey…"

"Hey," he said, "Nan's on her way home, but I'm taking a half-day, so it looks like I beat her."

"Oh, right," I said, "Well, I'll get going."

"Oh, hey," he said in a conciliatory tone of voice, "I don't know if Nan told you yet, but this little guy is going to be starting nursery school after Christmas, so we won't really need you to watch him anymore."

"Okay," I said, "No, she didn't say anything." I gave Leo a quick hug and left before the shock of basically having been fired bubbled up to the surface.

As I walked home, I sort of felt like crying, but I didn't. My thoughts were hotter and wetter than my tears would have been. Why hadn't Nan been the one to tell me? Why had it never even been mentioned to me that they were considering putting Leo in school? What sort of bullshit nursery school accepted children as young as Leo? I couldn't wait to read the pamphlet on that one… were they starting some sort of International Baccalaureate program for toddlers? No matter. I had experienced defeat before. I would make it work.

Over the next couple of days, I regrouped and began to search for jobs, once again trying to find solace in my dreams of revenge through unmitigated success. Mother had made herself busy with some new volunteer position at the arts council that she interpreted as *carte blanche* to completely overhaul the organization - she was constantly "volunteering" at the office in Plodis or lunching with someone to solicit donations. So, she was, thankfully, out of the house for large blocks of time and unable to opine on the state of my life. Looking at job descriptions can be one of the most depressing experiences known to mankind. In spite of my best intentions, my time at home devolved into watching television when my mother left and couldn't scold me, sitting and staring into space, and stress-eating the small amount that was possible in a kitchen full of flaxseed meal and dried fruit. I was in the middle of one of my famous staring spells after having read the worst kind of job listing, an entry-level one, when I heard the mail plop on the floor through the slot. It seemed the only civil thing to do would be to go and get it. There was never anything for me, but if I were lucky, the Nordstrom catalogue would have come and I could fritter away an hour passing editorial judgment on their newest cashmere and merino creations. There was a rather thick manila envelope on the bottom. Probably just another investment report for Mom and Dad, I thought. But then I noticed there was foreign postage on it and that it was actually addressed to me. Evidently from Eduardo, it contained a CD and a sealed envelope that said, "Listen first, read last." Always giving orders, that fuck. I gathered my things from the couch where I had been "working" and took it all to my room. My curiosity overrode my annoyance, as was often the case, and I put the CD in my computer to play it. At first I rolled my eyes. What cultural edification was I supposed to gain from listening to the same sounds of traffic he had played me in the pool house months ago? The sounds I heard now, though, were nothing like what I had expected. There was a melody, and after a while I recognized my own laugh, my voice singing a lullaby against more indiscernible creaks and groans. For as long as I had wished for a soundtrack to my life, I had never had one that was truly all my own. The sounds stopped and I sat there for a moment before ravenously tearing open the envelope. There was a handwritten note.

"I know you do not want to hear more of my opinions, that they upset you, but I have to tell you one more thing. Again and again, I tried to make this composition dark and grating, evidence of great industry's death and decline, but I could not escape your laugh, your love for the children. I know why you couldn't listen any longer to my criticisms of your home. In some way, you think home is built from the planks of your dreams, that home is the same thing as your soul, threatened by my denouncements; termites eating away all that you knew. Letting our childhood joys and struggles dictate our entire lives is not the same as belonging. This is a prison. Your life can be so much more than you think. Spend it waiting for the right situation and you will never discover the truth: the right situation is not based on ancestry, nor the rules you follow, nor dreams for love from those around you. You are the right situation. You are all you need. Travel to a place where you have no dreams outside yourself, where everything begins and ends in you. Make that your home.

P.S. If you ever need to travel to a real place, come to Argentina.

P.P.S. I can't stop thinking about you.

P.P.P.S. I love you."

If I had been operating at a normal level of brain function, I might have been confused, but I couldn't even process the thought that it would take for me to register confusion. I hadn't heard my mother come in the house, but she was now impatiently rapping on my bedroom door.

"Addie," she said, "We're due at the house to trim the tree any minute now, let's go."

I had forgotten about the obligatory tree trimming expedition to Gran and Pop's. They were back from Bermuda, then. I knew exactly how this evening would go. Gran would have had Dad or Palmer drive to a tree lot in the middle of nowhere and lug back an impractically large spruce that would only fit in the house's foyer. Gran and Pop would bring in the folding beach chairs from the garage and park in the middle of the marble-floor, Gran with a glass of wine, and Pop with a tumbler of scotch, and proceed to watch as the rest of us carried boxes of decorations up from the basement, and someone would haul out an old record player and put on the Beach Boys Christmas album. Upon arrival, I saw that in addition to all of these things being true, there was a card table holding a plastic-enclosed cheese tray. Gran and Pop had begun telling recycled Christmas memories.

Midway through this hallowed exercise, which was tolerable because of the cute children participating, Gran barked at Dad from her chair, "Bobby! We are definitely missing a box of ornaments."

My father, who was on his knees holding strands of Christmas lights around both of his arms like a skein of wool looked over at me.

"Addie, can you go find them?"

The basement of the house was not entirely dissimilar to the root cellar I pictured as the final resting place for my dreams. Basically a large stone cavern, it was populated almost entirely by shelving, illuminated by caged lights hanging from the ceiling. I walked over to the shelves where all the holiday decorations were kept, and sure enough, there was a huge box there labeled "ornaments." I had never really stopped and looked at what was here—the house had been in the family since it was built, so ostensibly nearly 100 years of Weston family memories lay in the copious boxes whose age could be told by the products they had housed before re-appropriation for storage. There was an old milk crate opposite me with "KAYE" scrawled on it in black marker. Whether because I wanted to know what the next chapter of my life might be or because I wasn't quite ready to go back upstairs and have my ears assaulted by the singular combination of "Little Saint Nick" and my grandmother's opinions on "twinkle lights," I edged it off the shelf and looked inside. It was a hodgepodge of records and old photographs. There was a record player right next to it on the shelf and I plugged it in and connected the biggest headphones I had ever seen to it. The records were all by someone named Les Baxter and had truly delightful titles like *The Soul of the Drums*, *Jungle Jazz*, *Wild Guitars*, and *The Fruit of Dreams*, which promised "the savage splendor of the fabled Aztec Empire," and "fascinating impressions of the Mysterious East." I finally settled on *Perfume Set to Music*. As dreamy crescendos and cinematic orchestra filled my ears, I began flipping through the photos. There were a few of Kaye from her days on the modeling circuit. A couple random childhood pictures of her and my father, a black and white wedding portrait of Gran, and then one that was much older, on cardboard, with the photographer's name and address printed on the bottom. It was of a young woman, in a long, almost Victorian wedding gown. Tall but petite, even the lace of her collar and sleeves seemed to hang off of her. Her dark hair was gathered into folded bundles of curls under a long veil. Her heart shaped face was beautiful, but her eyes looked almost weighed down, her tired gaze far away and hauntingly close at the same time. I turned the photo over, and it fell from my hand almost instantly, fluttering to the ground, landing face down, so that the name "Hestia" stared up at me. The song had ended and I stood frozen, listening to the sound of the needle skipping with each turn.

Kaye appeared at the doorway, evidently to figure out what the hell had happened to me, and I hurriedly pulled off the headphones and scooped the photo from the floor. She looked at me, a resigned look in her eyes, and walked over to where I was standing.

"You knew about her? You knew about the papers?" I asked, my voice shaking. She nodded.

"Does everyone know about her?"

"I don't know."

"Why did you keep her a secret?" I asked.

"I grew up, Addie. I got married, had Darwin, and this was something sad from the past that I didn't want to relate to anymore. She was a good friend to me before I went to New York. Her words made me believe it was okay to smoke cigarettes and cry on the terrace and that it was okay to escape. And, well, you already know how my foray into the big, bad world ended."

"So you just forgot about her?" She looked away.

"You never told Gran and Pop?"

"About the letters in the library? No. I mentioned her name once when they came to visit me at rehab."

"And?"

"They knew. They didn't want to talk about it. Dad having a secret suicidal mother isn't exactly the pride and joy of the

Weston name."

"And so you just gave up on her? Just left the letters there to be forgotten about again?"

"Listen, Addie. The day after I fought with them about it, Pop had a heart attack. Bet you didn't know that, huh? I didn't give up on her, I just didn't allow her to kill twice. Besides, I got better and stopped using, and went to therapy and got on mood regulators, and she didn't have a place in my happily ever after."

"And? You're happy?"

"What kind of silly question is that, Addie? Of course I'm happy." Even as she said it, her eyes flipped onto something inscrutable on the wall; her dismissiveness seemed fairly convincing evidence that happiness had become, to her, a relative term.

"I have to tell you something," I said.

"I know George is screwing someone at the conservatory too," she said, "It's just part of being an adult. You learn to be happy with what is. Now, come on upstairs before Gran gets suspicious and accuses you of stealing the silver."

She grabbed the box of ornaments and started up the stairs, as though nothing at all had just happened. I put the photo in my pocket and followed her, turning off the lights behind me.

The next day, Mom and Dad left the house early to go Christmas shopping. I sat at the breakfast nook and put Eduardo's CD into the player Mom kept in the kitchen. I placed each of Hestia's papers flat on the table in front of me, and Eduardo's letter too.

One by one, I read through them, and thought about my life over the past few months. I knew that in Ravine, I would always have a comfortable seat to sit in. I also knew, with increasing conviction, that I didn't want a great view of fireworks from comfortable surroundings, drinking Pellegrino and cuddling with a boy. I wanted to be the goddamn firework. I wanted to be high in the sky, blazing so brilliantly that I didn't care if anyone was even watching. Oh, you're on a diet, you run 5ks? That's cool. I'm a fucking firework. I don't need to be skinny or beautiful because you should simply appreciate my magnificence as is. Watch out for the pieces of me that are still burning as they rain down on your pale, bony shoulders. Oh, you're engaged and living in a penthouse and trying to decide where to honeymoon? You're in love? I don't need love, I'm a firework. I'll shine brilliantly with or without it.

I wanted to shine brilliantly with or without it. But I did need love, goddamn it. Love was all I had ever needed. And not some bullshit love that was the best somebody else could muster, either. Love I didn't have to second-guess. The only problem with being a firework, of course, was that fireworks are gone almost as soon as they begin. They're there for a minute and then they're gone and all you've got left is some generic memory of something that was just as nice as you had expected and that you could now forget. And that's what Hestia knew, I guess, that she couldn't last forever if she wanted to be different, more brilliant than the others. It seemed that I would just have to go somewhere where I didn't have to be some glowing ball of fire in the sky, because all I could be was myself. Myself wouldn't, for the first time, simply be a collection of other people's reactions to the world they'd been handed. It wouldn't even be my reaction to the world I'd been handed. I wouldn't have to think, alive in a world that didn't pretend to know every last inch of me. I could be myself in a place where they didn't even have fireworks because they just looked into people's eyes when they wanted to see something magnificent and beautiful. They didn't need to hear loud explosions because they listened to people's heartbeats, and they never had to watch a spectacle because instead of watching life, they were living it.

In Ravine, all of me that had been shown to the world was like a giant, human-shaped reflecting pool, a bunch of jagged, broken bits of mirror that had been stuck into me when I was still wet cement. My whole life, up until this point, had just been a series of distorted reflections. And maybe Eduardo had been able to see the two or three centimeters here or there where the mirror had fallen away and the cement had crumbled a bit—and there was a faint hint of flesh—of something breathing underneath. I didn't know what would happen in the next week, in the next month, in however many years remained before my death. I didn't know whether I loved Eduardo or liked him or would even be able to stand him after he spewed some arrogant, intellectual bullshit.

I didn't know whether one of my dream worlds would come to fruition or whether some sort of cranial natural disaster would raze every single dream world to the ground. But that wasn't the point—to protect the dream worlds, to go through life with an outer layer of mirrors in the hopes that, someday, I would catch some distorted reflection of happiness. The point was that I should be able to feel happiness and not just reflect it. I should be able to feel fear and anger and pride and hate all the time, not just when I decided to be an exploding firework against the night sky. I should be able to feel life, and not simply to dream of it. In order for this to occur, I would have to carry on through the uncertainty that made me so uncomfortable.

I went to my father's office and used the hidden key to open his locked desk drawer and retrieve my passport. I sat at his desk and wrote, on his writing paper, and with his fountain pen,

"Dear Mom and Dad,

Gone to Argentina. Will park my car in long-term parking. You have the spare. I'll be safe, don't worry.

Adelaide."

I packed a bag and drove myself to the airport and bought a one-way ticket. In a moment of indecision, I stopped walking toward the gate. Was this all a dreadful mistake? What on earth did I think was going to happen? Suddenly, without any warning, a little girl walking with her mother reached behind her, looking at me expectantly to take her hand. In spite of myself, I let a smile cross my lips. In her face, I saw Leo and I saw myself. I had worried for both of us that our experiences as children would condemn us to lives that were unchangeable. This was a chance for a new start of my own creation, a sort of living resurrection. I needed to prove to myself that my fate was not at the bottom of the lake with Hestia. It was somewhere in the sky, unthinkable and amazing.

As the plane took off, above the clouds, in brilliant sunlight, I fell asleep and dreamt of the root cellar, and the ending to the story that I had never considered. The dingy windows in the cellar broke and let the sunshine in, revealing that while all of the happinesses I had ever imagined were the size of small, dirty jars, I was destined for a happiness big enough to light up the entire sky.

I am sincerely grateful to each and every person who has supported me through this journey in any way. It took a village to make this book and you are all wonderful for participating in my process! That said, I thank:

- My parents, Ed and Carolyn, who love me in spite of this book.
- Abigail Corcoran, who encouraged me to follow my literary dreams louder than most.
- My siblings Chris, Amanda, and Emily, who will bitch at me to no end if I do not acknowledge them.
- Libby Freeze and Amelia Stefanac, who suffered through a year of me bouncing ideas off of them about a book they had not read.
- My bevy of editors and early readers, who are super cool folks:
  - Amanda Sweeney
  - Teresa Coda-Murray
  - Adrienne R. Liefeld, Lifelong Processed Sugar Provider to the Author
  - Amy Inman Villanueva, Leader of the Cool Kids Club
  - Lacey J. Davidson, Truth Seeker and Philosopher
  - Amelia Stefanac, Writer, Entrepreneur, and Food Enthusiast
  - Kristen Stevens, Commercial Photographer Who Will Someday be a Scientist.
  - Gabby Edlin
  - Emily Beach
  - Carolyn Beach
  - Marie Kirkeby
  - Kate Lewis
  - Lauren Sakioka
  - Carrie Schedler
  - Arika Lycan
  - Angie Gunnoe

www.ingramcontent.com/pod-product-compliance
Lightning Source LLC
Chambersburg PA
CBHW032000240626
47153CB00003B/1054